THE NAMELESS RESTAURANT

A COZY COOKING FANTASY

A HIDDEN
DISHES NOVELLA

Tao Wong

STARLIT PUBLISHING

Copyright

This is a work of fiction. Names, characters, businesses, places, events, and incidents are either the products of the author's imagination or used in a fictitious manner. Any resemblance to actual persons, living or dead, or actual events is purely coincidental.

No part of this publication may be reproduced, distributed, or transmitted in any form or by any means, including photocopying, recording, or other electronic or mechanical methods, without the prior written permission of the publisher, except in the case of brief quotations embodied in critical reviews and certain other non-commercial uses permitted by copyright law.

Books in the Hidden Universe

Hidden Dishes

The Nameless Restaurant

Hidden Wishes

A Gamer's Wish

A Squire's Wish

A Jinn's Wish

Table of Contents

PROLOGUE

There is a restaurant in Toronto. It's on a side street in the depths of Kensington Market, on the borders between old Chinatown and the market itself. Far from the towering skyscrapers of downtown and away from the cheap and easy eats frequented by the students of the University of Toronto.

Its entrance is announced only by a simple, unadorned wooden door, varnished to a beautiful shine but without paint, hidden beside dumpsters and a fire escape. There is no sign, no indication of what lies behind the door.

To find it, you have to know where to look, or you have to stumble upon it by pure luck. Reviews of the restaurant magically disappear, removed from internet directories and newspapers alike.

Directions grow garbled, words twisted and lost to the fogs of time and faulty memories.

If you do manage to find the restaurant, the décor is dated and worn. Homey, if one were to be generous. The service is atrocious, the proprietor a grouch. The regulars are worse, silent, brooding, and unfriendly to newcomers. There is no set menu, alternating with the whim and whimsy of the owner. The selection of wine and beer is sparse or non-existent at times, and the prices for everything outrageous.

There is a restaurant in Toronto that is magically hidden, whose service is horrible, and whose food is divine.

THIS IS THE STORY OF THE

NAMELESS RESTAURANT.

ONE
Golden Fried Rice

Midday light streamed in from the half-submerged windows facing the alleyway, adding to the soft illumination of incandescent light bulbs hanging from yellow chandeliers. The occasional metal pillar supporting the ceiling and the floor broke up the open floor plan of the restaurant, old wooden tables and threadbare, barely upholstered chairs. A dozen tables all told, some set against faded walls of grey concrete, the walls featuring a series of old black-and-white pictures of cities of a bygone age.

From the kitchen to the left of the entrance door, down from the staircase that took a right turn immediately upon entrance, the sound of someone chopping vegetables rang out rhythmically. White fluorescent light, harsh compared to the softer yellow of the dining room, shone from within, casting a long shadow of the cook. A bar with a half-dozen bar stools was set in front of the kitchen, a large open window showcasing the workings of the kitchen.

The smell of fresh-cut vegetables, boiling pots of stock, and a light floral scent of cleaning agent surrounded the man whose fingers danced across the chopping board, his knife wielded with practiced efficiency. Onions, garlic, celery, tomatoes, lettuce—all was chopped and prepped and set aside in rectangular metal containers for later use.

The peaceful scene was interrupted by the sudden thud of a body against the entrance doorway. A muffled grunt and yelp, as the door failed to give way or the knob to turn.

"Damn physical bodies." The feminine voice was loud and affronted as the doorknob rattled again. "Let me just…"

A slight pause, a buzz, and a yelp. "Aaargh! Who wards their damn door with a sixteenth level Archmage spell of forbiddance?"

A couple more thuds, as though someone was kicking the solid wooden door. The knife stopped moving, the cook's head rose as the knife was set gently against the chopping board. Full lips thinned for a moment, a hand reaching up to snatch the chef's cap off the head. The cook stalked out of the kitchen to the door, making a tiny gesture with his hand as he did so.

Lights grew brighter; a series of quiet clicks and humming rose up before ending. Another kick, the doorknob turned and the figure on the other side tumbled through the open doorway to stumble into the staircase railing.

The woman that tumbled in was raven-haired, with a prominent, aquiline nose and tanned skin. Her dark eyes flashed as she straightened up, rubbing the side of her ribs where she had knocked them. Behind her came a young Chinese man, looking somewhat amused at the woman's antics.

"Lily, the sign says 'closed'," the man said, exasperated. "You can't just go breaking in. If you're hungry, we could grab something down the street."

"No!" A pause, as the aforementioned Lily looked around and spotted the cook. She pointed an accusatory finger at him. "Ah hah! I found you, Mo Meng! Do you know how hard it was to find you?"

"Very."

"Exactly! This, this entire place is ridiculous." Lily spun around, gesturing about her. As she spun, light streamed from her hands, glowing sigils, characters and words appearing all across the wall. She pointed as she spoke. "There. Assyrian Numerology. Incan Blood Chant. Oh, they above. Is that a Malayalam Tribal Oration combined with a Japanese Poem Song?"

Now the young man was silent, his eyes greedily drinking in the glowing lights. On the other hand, Mo Meng looked less than impressed, moving his fingers a little again. The door behind the young man closed, blocking off the glowing sigils from the public outside.

"Exactly how much trouble did you get into?" Lily said. "Did you really need all this?"

"Obviously not," Mo Meng replied. "I needed more, if you found me."

Lily paused, staring at the tiny middle-aged Asian man, and then snapped her ingers. The glowing sigils, words and characters disappeared, leaving the room suddenly darker than ever.

"Whatever." She walked over to the counter, dragged out a bar stool and plopped her butt on it. "Feed me." Turning around, she beckoned to her companion. "Come down, Henry. I already turned off all the fatal wards."

Henry stared at the woman. His jaw worked for a few moments, and he looked between her and Mo Meng before he chose to come over and take a seat beside her. "You...you dragged me across the globe. Thrice. Through a raging viral magical pandemic, risking life and limb. All in search of this amazing, powerful archmage to ask him…to ask him to…."

"To cook for me!" Lily nodded. "Of course! Do you know how long I've dreamed of his food?"

Mo Meng glided across the floor, taking a place across from Lily on the other side of the bar. He eyed her and Henry for a second before he turned aside and fished out a teapot and a pair of teacups. Wandering over to a small electric heater, he put a clay pot on it and filled it with water from a glass bottle he found under the bar.

He said nothing, proceeding through the rest of the ritual. He rinsed the cups and teapot with the boiled water, pouring just a little of the hot water into the ceramic teapot to warm it further. Then, he moved to the small metal tin he had pulled from a desk, using wooden tongs to pick out a half-dozen delicate leaves. He dropped them into the pot after emptying it, before adding further hot water—now cooled from its boiling point—to the teapot.

Silence stretched, both Lily and Henry staring at the man's silent movements. Each action was like a well-choreographed dance, blending efficiency and a touch of flair, the minor extension of a hand, the flick of a wrist as he dropped the tea leaves.

It was hypnotizing, and in the stilling of the movement as they waited for the tea to steep, their breathing too lengthened and then settled.

Then, gently, he poured the tea into a strainer and another pot, the ceramic holding pot already warmed and washed. Carefully, across the two cups, he portioned the tea before setting the cups before the pair.

The smell of the tea leaves—delicate, fresh, grassy with the hint of the highland farms they had been plucked from, chosen from the freshest buds at the top of the trees and early in the spring—permeated the air.

Picking up the cup ever so gently, Henry sipped on the tea. His eyes closed, as the light and fresh taste of the tea leaves, the slight sweet and nutty flavor, permeated his tongue. The warmth of the cup and the size of it required him to sip only, but he realized only later that he had closed his eyes to truly savor the sensation.

By the time he had opened his eyes, Lily was done with her first cup, pouring herself a second from the ceramic holding pot.

"Good tea," Lily praised. "But that's not a good enough distraction. Cook for me!"

"And if I refuse?" Mo Meng said. "This is my restaurant. I cook when I want to, I serve who I wish." Shadows darkened all around the restaurant and Henry found himself shivering as Mo Meng—and what a name that was, Henry could not help but think. 'Nameless'. A true non-name for sure—glared at Lily.

"Then I'll keep coming back. Every night." She raised a finger. "For one whole century. Every. Night."

Mo Meng shut his eyes and exhaled, loudly. Then, almost plaintively, as the shadows receded, he said. "I'm not even open, you know."

"It's fine. Whatever you have lying around will do," Lily replied, brightening immediately.

"You're going to be the death of me." He picked up the hot water kettle, dropping it on the table and gesturing to the teapot. "You remember how?" At Lily's nod, he continued. "The tea is best on the second steeping. Throw it out after the third."

Then, having said his piece, he returned to his kitchen, leaving a bemused youngster and his companion seated outside.

Mo Meng surveyed the interior of his kitchen, the half-completed prep work that he had been forced to abandon, the ingredients that were laid out before him. He frowned, considering his options given what was on hand, and then the pair outside. Choosing a dish was not just a matter of what he had on hand, but also what suited his customers.

Though he somehow doubted that Lily intended to pay.

He dismissed concerns about payment, even as he strolled over to his fridge. Considering all that he had available, and what he intended to do for tonight, his best option was not to touch his current stores, but the stores he had intended for himself.

A little rooting around the big metal refrigerator yielded the metal container filled with day-old rice. He extracted the entire thing, picking up a small spoon and testing the rice before nodding to himself. It was not perfect—letting it warm a little before he began the cooking process would have been best—but it would do.

A flick of his hand put a spell on it, to bring its temperature up faster. Not too much, of course, because then the rice would burn before it was cooked, but too cold and he would have to leave the ingredients to dry out while warming it all.

Cooking, like life, was a balancing act. Prior preparation ensured the best result, but magic made for a suitable shortcut.

Next, the other ingredients. The wok he used was placed on the burners and left to heat, as the gas-fired burner turned on with a click of the electric starter. The wok itself was an old piece of equipment, cast iron with a pair of small rectangular handles on either side for gripping. Both the inside and outside were blackened from years of use, tempered over countless flames, the ingredients of hundreds of dishes soaking into it.

He grabbed at the other ingredients quickly, pulling their metal containers over, including the bountiful supply of eggs that had been set aside earlier.

Each egg was large and round, their light brown coating perfect. He cracked open four in rapid succession into a simple porcelain mixing bowl, a quick dash of salt added before he began the process of beating the eggs till the mixture had a silky, golden texture to it. He stopped when that happened, not wanting to overbeat the egg.

A glance at the wok showed that it had begun to heat to the appropriate warmth, so he added a squirt of sunflower oil. He dribbled it around the edges, swirling the wok about to ensure it was properly coated, and then went back to beating the egg to ensure a proper consistency.

Then, garlic into the pan. He listened to the hiss and sizzle as it hit the pan, stirring the garlic a little as he waited for it to simmer and crisp. When it was finished, he used the chuan, the long-handled metal spatula, to extract the garlic, setting it aside in a slotted bowl so that any excess oil would drip off. Then the onions were added.

Those he waited to turn translucent—not long at all, not with the temperature involved.

While he waited, the beaten eggs were added to the warmed rice. He mixed the entire thing together swiftly, knowing that if he waited too long, the rice would grow soggy. As it was, a few quick and practiced motions broke up the rice, each grain splitting away from the other. It took multiple washes of the rice on the day before and proper control of water to ensure that each rice grain was individually separated, rather than clumping together.

Once the egg was in, further wet ingredients were added. A dash of high-grade soya sauce from a small batch creator in the Fejian province. Light on salt, heavy on the umami. Then he tipped the bottle of Shaoxing rice wine over the dish, sesame oil to add its powerful fragrance, and white pepper.

Mixed together, the entire combination was added to the translucent onions. Immediately upon hitting the hot wok, the smell of burning alcohol and the slight sweetness of the wine rose up, along with the intense smell of the sesame oil.

One hand held the bowl, the other scooped and dumped rice, stir-frying the rice in the wok. Occasionally, he would dip downwards to touch the edge of the wok to flip or stir the rice or adjust the flame heat, ensuring good *wok hei*.

This part was now all skill, for the goal was to mix rice and egg together in such a way that each grain was covered by the golden mixture as well as cooked so that no single grain was dried out or the rice clumped together from the wet ingredients.

His hand turned, shifting the dish over and over again, the flames under the wok burning hot, throwing additional shadows from beneath as it heated the dark, cast-iron wok.

The smell of the cooking rice rose up, tickling his nostrils. A quick eyeball of the meal and he turned off the burners with a flick of his free hand, pulling a pair of shallow, curved plates toward him. He grabbed the long-handled wok ladle from its place hanging to the side of the cooking station and swiftly ladled the mixture onto the plates. He dropped the compact half spheres onto the center and cleared out every single grain of rice from the wok.

Leaving the cooking implement to cool, he extracted a couple of sprigs of cilantro to place on top of the golden rice, along with a sprinkling of chopped slices of crispy garlic. Then he wiped down the dishes before bringing the plates to the dining room.

The entire process took less than five minutes.

"Gods, that smells good," Henry Tsien said, his mouth watering as he sniffed at the air like a dog. He listened to the clang of the spatula as it struck the wok, a small smile crossing his face. "What do you think he's cooking us?"

"Something cheap. And easy," Lily said, confidently.

"That's…. not nice."

"He's not nice," Lily replied, still with a smile on her lips. "But it'll still be good."

"You seem very confident in him," Henry said, then cocked his head to the side. "Also, how, exactly, do you know him or even were certain he was alive? I mean, you were trapped for decades and he doesn't look a day over forty."

"Looks can be deceiving, haven't I told you before?" Lily said.

"I checked for glamours. There are none," Henry replied immediately. "Though that seems to be about the only kind of magic that isn't present. There's more kinds of magic in here than I can name." He turned from his consideration of his upcoming meal to survey the walls again, a slight gleam in his eyes as he cast a spell to give him sight over the magic that Lily had revealed earlier.

He knew she had done it for his sake. She didn't need to make it visible to make her point, or see it.

After all, the jinn was magic itself. Quite literally, in a way.

Before the woman could answer, Mo Meng exited the kitchen, wandering through the open doors with both plates in hand. He placed the golden rice topped with the fresh, lustrous cilantro and the golden-brown garlic chips before the pair, fishing beneath the counter before extracting two sets of rolled-up utensils for the pair of them.

Immediately, Henry's mouth began watering even more heavily. He spun the barstool around so that he was fully focused on the meal, leaning forwards to breathe in deep the enticing smells. The hint of cilantro, the strong fried garlic and the smell of the egg-covered rice made him gulp.

"Fried rice?" Lily said, only sounding mildly disappointed. "There's not even prawns, or anything in it!"

"It's not just fried rice," Henry said, unwrapping the utensils and taking the spoon in his hand. He gently pushed against the rice, the spoon sliding between the grains without hesitation, the rice parting like water before a dipping hand. "It's golden fried rice."

"It's rice. Fried. What's the difference?" Lily said, wrinkling her nose.

If Henry had not known her better, he would have called her a brat. As it was, he did. And so, he said it loud. "Stop teasing him. And say thank you." Then, echoing his action with words, he smiled at Mo Meng. "This smells great."

"Food is meant to be admired, yes. But also, eaten." Having made his point, Mo Meng turned away and wandered back into the kitchen to continue with his preparations.

"A man of few words," Henry muttered. Then, shrugging, he lifted the spoonful he had made and placed it in his mouth.

The moan he next made was not gracious at all. It echoed through the room, as the delicious flavors combined in his mouth. Each grain was perfectly cooked, the egg-covered rice perfectly separating in his mouth as he chewed on it, the tart taste of the Shaoxing wine combining with the fragrant sesame oil, all of it dissolving in his mouth as the added umami and saltiness of the soya sauce tipped the dish over. He chewed, swallowed and was reaching for another spoonful before he realized it.

This time, a spoonful of rice and the garlic chip went into his mouth together. He bit down, the crunch of the chip a pointed contrast to the soft and savory rice, the slight spiciness of the chip combining with the white pepper in a further explosion of taste.

Another groan, but this time, he realized; it had been echoed.

Looking over, he saw that Lily had half consumed her meal, her head bent down and her mouth wide open as she shoveled the dish into her mouth.

"Not complaining anymore, are you?" Henry said, after swallowing.

The raven-haired woman just glared at him, before chewing and gulping down her latest mouthful. Then, still looking at Henry, she stabbed her dish and picked out another mouthful of the golden rice, raising it to her mouth and taking a bite.

He smirked, before turning his attention to his own dish. He would not put it past Lily to steal his food, though her gluttony had never been a factor before. Sure, she had a healthy appetite—which, when you considered the fact that she was a purely magical being was both fascinating and annoying—but she had never been gluttonous.

Not till now, at least.

Sooner than he had expected, Henry found his dish empty before him. Every single speck of rice was gone, picked over by himself. The same could be said for Lily's bowl. Placing the utensils on the shallow plate, he pushed it away from him and stared at the open window into the kitchen where the rhythmic noises of a knife at work continued to emanate.

"Thank you for the meal," Henry called out to the man who worked religiously, ignoring them both.

Then turning to Lily, he lowered his voice. "So what now?"

To his surprise, Lily was on her feet, her mouth wiped and a smile on her face. "Now? We go. We'll be back for dinner."

She pitched the last sentence loud enough that Mo Meng, within the kitchen, was forced to hear it. He looked up at her through the open counter, and just offered a simple nod before he returned to his work. Henry frowned, gesturing at the empty bowls.

"Uhh, how much do we owe you?" he said.

"Don't be silly. We don't have to pay. That was a meal for a friend," Lily said.

"I don't…"

"It's fine." Then, as though feeling a little guilty, she added. "We'll pay for dinner later. And don't be in such a rush to pay him, anyway."

"Why?" Henry said, suddenly guarded. After all, payment—receiving or taking it—could be dangerous in the supernatural world. Especially when dealing with the strange, like the fae. Though few of the old fae were around with their idiosyncratic views. Still, Lily was a trouble magnet.

"Because he's a real cheat. His dishes are really expensive." So saying, Lily proceeded to flounce out of the restaurant, leaving Henry to stare after her.

He looked back to Mo Meng and saw the man make a small gesture, shooing him out. Defeated, Henry hurried after his master and friend, hoping she hadn't just disappeared on him.

Again.

Still, even if she did, he was certain he'd find her again tonight. Somehow, he knew she was not going to miss dinner tonight.

TWO
Kelly and the Patrons

Only when the pair had left did Mo Meng finally breathe a small sigh of relief. He looked at the vegetables he had prepped, the noodles he had set aside to soak and part, the mollusks he needed to deshell, and made a face. He had a lot of work left to do and only a single pair of hands.

For a brief moment, temptation ran through him. It would be a simple spell, to conjure a couple of additional helpers. Spells, dozens of them, ran through his mind. Spirit Helpers carried the memories of their past lives, allowing him to call upon the greatest chefs in the world.

But they were draining, and piercing the void had a tendency to weaken the shroud, leaving it open to additional, unwanted hauntings.

Ingrid's Helping Hands created multiple, semi-autonomous hands that he could manipulate, just like his own. However, they lacked the full sensory input of his own hands and required him to split his attention. Another spell could help with that, allowing him to run parallel thoughts, but it did nothing for the lack of feedback.

So many spells, so many ways to make this work easier. Then, with a firm shake of his head, he pushed temptation aside. The kitchen was his domain, his refuge. Outside of mini-catastrophes like his most recent guest, he refused to use magic to make the job easier.

Good food required time, care, precision and most of all, love.

None of which magic helped with.

Not really.

Silence descended upon the kitchen once more, and Mo Meng smiled to himself, lulled into the quiet serenity of work. Vegetables were chopped, meat taken out, sliced and seasoned, stock started for the next day. So much of cooking in his kitchen was dedicated to planning for the next day, the next week, the next month.

Stock, set to a slow boil with bags of chicken feet as the base; meant to be reduced down over hours so that the collagen and tendons and skin broke apart, the scum skimmed off to leave just the rich fifth flavor, umami.

Not for today, but for one of his most popular evenings—ramen night.

Meat, seasoned carefully with salt and pepper before being taken to hang inside the cold, temperature-controlled cubicle, fans carefully positioned to allow a constant flow of air within, to be aged for twenty-eight to thirty days. Those slices of meat would be for special occasions, for a few optimal dishes.

Livers, for the next days, set to soak in tubs of milk to leach out the bitter flavor of blood. Tofu, pressed downwards by a light stone, would be extracted later and placed within a bath of sauces to absorb the flavor, to be used later today for the meal, after being deep-fried with wheat germ and nutritional yeast as a meat substitute for the vegetarians.

Preparations, for tonight and tomorrow and the week ahead, one after the other. He breathed in, the ritual of preparation taking over, a different kind of magic that allowed time to pass by without a care, until the noise of the door opening once more alerted him.

Mo Meng looked up from where he was finishing the washing up, hands never stopping as he scrubbed the cutting board down, to spot the latest newcomer, relaxing only when he noticed who it was.

"Hey boss-man, there something going on that I wasn't told about?" The voice was high and happy, the speaker bouncing in with a smile on her face as brown eyes glinted beneath pink hair.

"Unexpected guests," Mo Meng said.

"Mmm…. So I see." Passing by where the pair had been seated at the counter to stare within, the young lady pushed the pair of barstools in, positioning them in their proper places. She then paused, sniffing audibly and then peering around the room. "They the reason you behind?"

"I'm not behind. Meal preparations are complete," Mo Meng said, arms crossing defensively.

"Sure, sure. But normally, you'd have the staff meal ready and be regaling me about the latest dish," she said.

"Kelly, sometimes I wonder if you forget who's the employer and who the employee here," he said, mock glaring at her.

She grinned back just as cheekily before pounding lightly on the table. "Food, food, food!"

"Fine…" Mo Meng said, with a long-suffering sigh. A few minutes later, after the use of the same wok—washed lightly with a little soap and a lot of water—he returned with a plate of fried noodles, depositing the dish before the woman.

She grinned, sticking her hands together and declaring, "Itadakimasu!"

Mo Meng rolled his eyes, leaving the anime lover alone to enjoy the food as he finished prep. Within minutes, she had inhaled the dish and had returned to deposit the empty plate and chopsticks behind, before starting the process of setting up the restaurant to take customers.

That consisted of turning on the few other lights in the building, wiping down and rearranging chairs as necessary, double-checking on the quantity of napkins, utensils and other miscellaneous items before doing the last, most onerous chore. Visiting the washrooms and cleaning those out.

In the meantime, Mo Meng made his way to the simple chalkboard at the side of the bar that separated the drinks section and kitchen from the dining room, wiping off yesterday's specials and scribbling today's menu on it.

Dinner Menu

Char Kuey Teow
(Pork, Chicken or Vegetarian)

Curry Laksa
(Chicken or Vegetarian. Includes prawns)

Golden Fried Rice

Dessert

Sago with Gula Malacca and fruit
toppings

Drinks

Fresh Coconut Juice

Soybean Milk

Once he was done, Mo Meng stepped back and stared at the dishes written on his wall. After a moment, he nodded in satisfaction and turned around to glare down at Kelly, who had snuck up on him and was standing directly behind his back. He showed no sign of being surprised, though, just looking at her with a raised eyebrow.

"You really are no fun," Kelly said, stepping to the side with a sniff and staring at the menu. "We doing Southeast Asian again?"

"Malaysian, specifically," Mo Meng said. "Make sure to clarify if someone asks. Not Singaporean laksa, which is a little too watery, but Malaysian curry laksa."

"Right. Malaysian." Kelly frowned in concentration, then rattled off the ingredient list for each of the dishes, one after the other. Mo Meng listened with his head cocked to the side, correcting her once in a while before she was done.

"So, ripe honeydew, mango, coconut or slices of cempadak for the sago, all with coconut milk and gula malacca, right?" Kelly waited for Mo Meng to nod before she wrinkled her nose in disappointment. "No *goreng pisang*?"

"Weren't you the one who complained that eating all that fried food was making you fat just last week?" Mo Meng said, teasingly.

"That's different! That was a whole meal." Kelly pouted. "You know I love the fried bananas. Especially when accompanied with your vanilla ice cream."

Mo Meng shuddered theatrically. "Heathen. All of you, heathens for adding ice cream to a perfectly fine dish."

"You're just stuck in your ways."

"I put the fruit toppings on, didn't I?" He gestured back to the board. "Not that there's anything wrong with just plain. And you should offer that too!" He waggled his fingers at Kelly who nodded somberly. "All right, best get the rest ready. I need to start prepping. We've got our usual outside."

Kelly nodded, taking his assertion without question. She watched as he walked back into the kitchen, stopping at the open doorway for a moment to turn back and reply, softer.

"Be careful tonight. Make sure you wear the necklace. Things might get…strange."

"Strange as in people orgasming eating or strange like…" She waggled her fingers.

"That kind."

"Ah…." Kelly wrinkled her nose, touching the hard lump under her blouse reactively. "Right." Then brightening up the next moment, she sauntered back to the front doors, pausing only long enough to review the room one last time before throwing the door open for the waiting guests.

"Welcome to the Nameless Restaurant!"

The first man to walk in was just over five feet three tall and nearly as wide, it seemed. He sported a neatly trimmed black beard, a contrast to the white mop of hair and lined face. Clad in a rolled-up, plaid workman's shirt and dirty, working jeans, every step of his heavy work boots resounded off the concrete stairs he descended. Once he was inside, he snatched his hat off his head, nodding in response to Kelly's cheerful greeting before stomping down the remaining steps to make his way to the counter.

Kelly did not even blink as the customer blew past her, nor was she surprised as another lady glided in behind the older man. In direct contrast to the earlier gentleman, she was in an elegant sable evening gown, one more suited for a fine dining establishment than the Nameless Restaurant. Discreet accessories glittered in the artificial light, diamond bracelets, a pair of beautiful rings, small, discreet earrings and a golden necklace subtly drawing the eye and completing her ensemble.

Designer purse in hand, the lady took a seat at a table away from the older gentleman, positioning her chair so that she could see both the kitchen and the entrance at the same time. Immediately after sitting, she began to study the menu just as intently as the older man.

The final impatient customer arrived later, moving slowly as he crossed the threshold. He let out a little shudder as he did so, glancing upwards at the hidden glyphs before stepping all the way in and straightening himself to his full height, towering over Kelly at his full seven feet.

Moments later, he reached down and grabbed her in his arms, lifting her off the ground and hugging her close.

"Kelly!"

"Let me go, you big oaf!" Hands held to the side, she smacked him till she was released. "And it's good to see you too. Where have you been?"

"Clan business," the big man rumbled, looking about. He spotted the larger than normal seats located near the back of the room and walked over, glancing into the kitchen and shouting a greeting to Mo Meng as he did so.

"So loud. Why are you always so loud!" the elegant woman complained, her voice cultured and delicate. "Can you not be quieter, Clan Leader Jotun?"

"No."

"Kelly." A hand rose, waving the waitress over to the older, shorter gentleman seated by the bar. When she arrived, he pointed to the menu with the same hand that waved her over. "I have decided."

"Of course." Kelly whipped out a small notebook and pen, looking attentive. "What will you have?"

"I have decided to have one of everything."

"Did you even have to tell her, Tobias?" the woman spoke again, rolling her eyes. "You order one of everything every time."

"Good decisions take time. Good decisions require proper consideration," Tobias rumbled. "Not all of us can be as flighty as you, Eleanor. Or have you changed your name again?"

"Flighty…" Eleanor's eyes narrowed. "At least some of us know when to let loose, unlike you stone-brained…"

Kelly, having swept into the kitchen to deposit the order slip, came hurrying over, interposing herself between the two customers. She smiled widely, hefting pen and paper. "And what will you be ordering, Lady M?"

The blonde woman PAUSED, her attention drawn back to the board before she smiled. "I shall try the Curry Laksa and two orders of your sago." She paused, leaning forwards. "What kind of toppings?" After listening, she added. "Mango and plain, if the chef himself recommends it. And the sugar cane."

Kelly wrinkled her nose at the addition of the plain, but she chose not to comment, hurrying over to Jotun before she deposited the order.

"Four plates of the Char Kuey Teow. Extra, extra spicy," he rumbled, determinedly. "And I'll have two of the Golden Rice too. Water only."

"Four Char Kuey Teow, two Golden Rice and water. I'll get the order right in!" Kelly chirped, sweeping away to drop off the food orders. Then, casting a glance at the doorway which still stood empty, she entered the kitchen, looking around for the drinks.

"Soy bean in the fridge," Mo Meng said, not even looking up as he heated a pair of woks on the gas burner. "I'll prep the coconut juice in a moment."

Kelly nodded, taking his word for it as she pulled open the refrigerator and found the glass pitcher containing the pale white, almost milk-like drink. She lifted the lid a little, pouring it into the tall, clear serving glass and smiling a little as the slightly sweet smell of pressed soy bean struck her nose. Moments later, she had the drink deposited in front of Tobias and a cup of water before Jotun.

Tobias picked up the drink, turning it from side to side to stare at the clear, strained liquid before sniffing at it. Like Kelly, he noticed the smell of sugar and the slightly nutty, milky smell of the drink. Then, raising the glass to his lips, he sipped.

The first thing he noticed was the earthy flavor, driven by the creamy, slightly nutty taste of the liquid. It was refreshing in the way a glass of cold milk could be, but without the film of thick creaminess that milk often left behind; the entire drink having been strained multiple times to remove any sediment. The taste was enhanced by the sweetener added to it, accenting the mild and invigorating flavor.

Before he realized it, Tobias had drunk half the glass down, a smile pulling his lips upwards. Tension that he carried in his shoulders relaxed, as he leaned into the back of his bar stool and waited for the rest of his meal, watching as Mo Meng worked his magic within.

Inside the kitchen, Mo Meng had turned to one of the cupboards beneath his kitchen and extracted two young coconuts. Moving over to the garbage bin, he flipped the lid open, grabbing the cleaver that hung nearby off its hook. A series of quick, precise cuts for each coconut as he rotated it shaved the outer shell away. Then, a single horizontal slice took the tops off, leaving a small opening in the green coconut for a straw to be added, along with a long teaspoon. Placing the pair of coconuts aside for Kelly to retrieve, Mo Meng made his way to the woks.

Already, the pans had heated up sufficiently. A quick glance upwards to check on the tickets, before he began the process of cooking. The golden fried egg rice required his full concentration, and three orders was one too many.

Years of practice had clarified a few things for Mo Meng. Firstly, there was an optimal amount of beaten egg-coated rice that could be added to a wok. You could increase the size of the wok, increase the flame and heat to distribute the temperature a little more; but the egg fried rice had a tendency to dry out in parts, overcooking the egg and making the golden 'paint' flake off rather than covering each grain in its iridescent shell.

On the other hand, in a regular-sized wok, if you increased the amount of rice, you encountered the other problem of the rice clumping together. Rather than being able to properly distribute heat across the meal and part the rice grains individually by stirring them around, clumps would form from the clustered and crowded rice.

Then, instead of each individual grain being perfectly moist with a layer of savory goodness, you received clumped, slightly too moist mouthfuls.

Of course, another chef might cook the same portion size and then divide the portion sizes into three dishes rather than two. Smaller quantities, higher prices, and you could call yourself a luxury experience.

Just the thought made Mo Meng's lips curl in disgust.

He was no American either, offering portion sizes that were guaranteed to make his patrons overweight. Though, at this point, his attention drifted to his regular patrons and he found himself laughing a little—silently—at his own morals.

It was not as though any of his regular customers were normal either.

All through his idle musings, his hands had never stopped moving. Rice was added, stirred and cooked, fragrant eggs and sesame oil drifting through the kitchen before the meals were carefully portioned. Then, another swirling addition, before he did the same again but for a smaller portion this time.

In minutes, three dishes had made their appearance, the first two whisked away to the customers. In that time, another patron had wandered in and sat down. Another order was added to his growing list, Mo Meng spending a moment to pin it above his head, flicking his gaze down the details before moving on.

Kelly scurried in, picking up the soybean milk that had been deposited in the refrigerator, pouring a cup before hurrying back to her customer, and finally, Mo Meng found time to work on the other dishes.

THREE
Char Kuey Teow

Char Kuey Teow was a hybrid dish created in Southeast Asia, formed from the combination of Chinese and Malaysian cultures. The stir-fried rice noodle dish had been created by fishermen and cockle-gatherers in the southern maritime regions, and grew in popularity due to its high level of nutrients, energy and bountiful taste.

The flat rice noodles used to prepare the dish—the kuey teow—could easily be acquired these days in any well-stocked

Asian supermarket. In its commercial form, the noodles need only be soaked in water, allowing the compressed and mildly dried-out dish to soak up the water and separate the noodles themselves before use. Such noodles were used in a variety of other fried and noodle dishes, thrown in to provide necessary carbohydrates and the silky feel of the rice noodles themselves.

Mo Meng, of course, eschewed the idea of purchasing commercial noodles. Though the quality level had grown significantly over the decades, leaving most of the commercial-grade noodles acceptable for most uses, 'most' was not sufficient for him.

Instead, to prep for tonight's dinner, he had prepared the rice noodles himself. The process had begun with the purchase of specialized rice that had a significant gluten content. Of course, Mo Meng was not a masochist, so he had made full use of both the machines at hand and a slight touch of his magic to grind down the rice to form the rice flour he needed.

After that, tapioca starch—his own personal preference compared to the more common corn starch that he felt diluted the taste a little too much—was added along with a touch of salt and water. In this case, he used spring water from the Junan district, where the water was a touch sweet and lacked the iron afterbite other water might have.

Mixed together, the mixture was then added to a flat, lightly oiled pan before he put them into his industrial steamer. Multiple pans were created and prepped in this manner, carefully stirred to ensure that the rice mixture never settled. The milky white noodles, once steamed, would tighten and cook on the pans.

Peeled off the pans, the noodles were then brushed with oil and sliced into long, five-centimeter by one-centimeter strips before being stored in the fridge for use today. Tens of the pans were steamed and the flat, rice noodle strips created, each bundle carefully packaged in plastic wrap for use.

Use today, that was.

Of course, that was just the first step in creating a proper dish of char kuey teow.

The next important step was the creation of the sauce. Each cook had their own recipe and portions for the sauce, the main ingredients including soy sauce, dark soy sauce, oyster and fish sauce, and then sugar and pepper. Those were the basics, though Mo Meng had made minor adjustments to the basic dish.

Firstly, white pepper was substituted for the black pepper others used, the lighter taste of the white pepper blending better in his own view. Mo Meng also preferred to ignore the addition of fish sauce, preferring to use the more traditional fresh and bloody cockles to give the authentic fishy flavor.

Finally, he adjusted the portions of dark and light soy sauce, leaning towards a richer soy sauce from the northern regions of China and a lighter soy sauce from Canton. Both, he felt, allowed for a bolder and more complex flavor, especially paired with the oyster sauce and pepper.

Once created, the urn of kuey teow sauce could be stored for weeks at a time in the refrigerator, so Mo Meng had a tendency to create big batches to allow for multiple themed cooking nights like this, rather than repeat the process over and over again. It was another reason he preferred using fresh cockles rather than fish sauce, since the addition of fish sauce—even commercially created ones—had a tendency to embitter the sauce after a period of time, even when it was refrigerated.

All that was simple prep—beyond, of course, the chopping, warming and extraction of the Chinese sausage, the fresh cockles, the deveined large freshwater prawns, and the cleaning of the bean sprouts—before the dish was ready to be served.

However, like most dishes created for cooking on the streets, while the meal was heavy on preparations beforehand; the actual cooking time was quick. In fact, speed of cooking and the use of proper temperature and heat was all-important for the final product, as any true connoisseur would tell you.

The first and most important secret about cooking good char kuey teow was in the oil used. Many new restaurants, in the interest of health-consciousness, chose to shift away from the traditional method, utilizing vegetable or, even more scandalously, olive oil. None of that was actually conducive to the proper cooking of the dish, for at the required high temperatures olive oils—and scandalously, butter—would smoke, adding an unseemly flavor to the dish. Vegetable oils—sunflower, grapeseed and the like—were better in that regard, but removed a rather important vector of taste.

No, the traditional and still the best method was to utilize pork lard—rendered pork fat—as the base oil. You swirled it around the wok with a quick flick of the scoop, letting it begin to smoke as the flames under your wok worked at high heat. Then, the first item to go in was the prawns, thrown into the lard to crackle and cook. Dried off for the most part, with just a tiny amount of moisture, the prawns would hiss and shrink, curling in on themselves as they gained a light pink veneer, before one flipped them over to the other side and repeated the process.

Then, next, quickly before the prawns overcooked in the heat, you threw in the chopped garlic, letting it sear on the wok bottom with the prawns. A teaspoon's worth—unless, of course, your customer was a garlic fan like the Clan Leader—before you moved on. You had to do this fast, for the high heat beneath the wok ensured the garlic seared and cooked quickly, chopped into tiny cubes as it was. Another quick dip into the other side, to add a small handful of deep-fried, crispy pork crackling to ensure that the powerful aroma and silkiness was kept.

The flat, long kuey teow noodles went in next. The damp noodles released a puff of steam when they hit the wok, even as the wok spatula in Mo Meng's experienced hand kept them stirring. High temperatures—the *wok hei* that was intrinsic to the dish—meant that everything had to be cooked quickly, including the addition of the kuey teow seasoning, which was ladled in.

This was where experience came in, for the amount and quantity of seasoning had to be judged for each dish based on the amount of moisture in the noodles, the heat of the wok, and the quantity of the dish. Too much and the noodles would not char properly, too little and the dish would be flat, lacking any seasoning and taste.

More stirring, while the noodles coated with the kuey teow sauce were heated and charred. Chinese sausage was now added, only a few slices at the start. This always released another burst of fragrant aroma as the fat in the Chinese sausages—half-cooked and dried—released itself into the air. Eyeing the concoction, Mo Meng added another small dash of sauce to the dish before tossing in the pre-cooked fish cake. Again, only a half-dozen slices went in, to provide moisture and a different, more rubbery texture.

Then, the dish was nearly done.

The first plates went to the Clan Leader, the portions in the wok sufficient to provide for two dishes. Extra spicy meant added chili paste, pre-prepared in large batches and then refrigerated. The spice in the chili actually kept the seasoning fresh and therefore it could be stored out of the fridge, though for safety's sake Mo Meng rarely did so.

One big scoop with the edge of the wok spatula before it was added to the dish, the blob of chili mixed around aggressively to ensure that it broke apart. Then, the noodles and prawns were flipped onto the chili, spreading the redness all over the dish. Knowing his customer, Mo Meng had added enough that the normally light brown colour with a dash of red for a 'normal' char kuey teow dish had changed, becoming a bright, fire-engine red from the chili paste.

The big man had big taste.

Once the moisture and the chili had burned away and mixed into the dish properly, added along with a small handful of bean sprouts whose release of moisture kept the noodles from drying out too much, the final steps were ready.

The wok was shifted sideways, raised upwards in one direction and the noodles pushed to the side. An egg was scooped up, cracked and added to the revealed section of the wok, the yolk broken and spread across the egg white. When it was half-cooked—a matter of seconds under the high heat—the entire dish was once again mixed together, layering the half-cooked egg over it.

Then came the blood cockles, a rare find in these parts. This was where magic was of use, since getting the best, freshest versions of these required suppliers from southeast Asia itself. Thankfully, minor teleportation spells were simple enough to conduct, when you had a warded and fixed room. Simple, that was, for a mage of his caliber.

Blood cockles were best eaten half-cooked, which meant that they had to be added near the end. Another series of flips, and then finally the last ingredients were thrown in, diagonally sliced green chives and more bean sprouts.

Another couple of breaths, just enough to warm and sear the vegetables, and then the dish was done. Plates were grabbed, the char kuey teow ladled in, and then the plates were set aside on the counter before him, even as more pork lard was added to the same wok to begin the heating process for the next two dishes.

All in all, it took less than five minutes to cook, with Kelly already hurrying over, ready to grab the warm dishes and serve them to the Clan Leader.

Two plates of cherry-red char kuey teow, so spicy that Kelly made sure to hold the dish away from her body as she brought it over to the Clan Leader. The big man had just finished both dishes of golden rice, sipping on the plain water that had been served to him to help cleanse his palate, when she arrived with the dishes, placing both in front of the man.

"Ah, good. Perfectly spiced, as always," Jotun said, eyeing the red color with a big grin. He fished around in the utensil rack, pulling out a pair of chopsticks before tugging the first dish to him. Chopsticks dipped into the dish, extracting a mouthful of brightly-colored noodles, Jotun already having ignored the young lady who had deposited it.

Raising the mixture of noodles, bean sprouts and a single slice of green chives, he popped it into his mouth. The first thing Jotun noticed was not the spice, but the silky mouth-feel that the lard cooked and coated noodles brought to his lips as they passed into his mouth. Then, of course, came the spice.

Homemade chili paste, ground down from large red chilies grown in northern India, with its fiery zing made its presence known. Opening his mouth a little to blow outwards, Jotun hissed in delight as his tongue was set on fire.

Beneath the heat, though, were the other complex flavors. The crispiness and slight charring from the noodles, the textural differences in the silkiness of the noodles along with the crispiness of the burnt edges, the saltiness and umami from both kinds of soy sauce, all combined in his mouth. As he bit down, the bean sprouts crunched between his teeth, adding another textural difference, even as Jotun chewed and swallowed, sweat appearing on his brow.

Chopsticks dipped again, gripping a springy prawn this time along with another mouthful of noodles. He bit and chewed, the springiness of the perfectly cooked prawn bringing the slight sweetness and savoriness into his mouth, a small trickle of saltwater mixing with the spice. He chewed on the noodles and the prawn quickly, savoring the combination of taste before going back for more.

Another mouthful of noodles and bean sprouts, and then finally he struck the blood cockles. A shellfish delicacy known mostly to those in the maritime regions of southeast Asia, the red-tinted meat blended perfectly with the red of his own dish.

The red-colored meat of the cockles had a salty, oceanic flavor, with a touch of sweetness in it that cleansed the spice and noodle taste from his mouth almost immediately. The cockle itself was half-cooked, allowing Jotun to slice through the tender flesh with ease with his big teeth, chewing the mouthful together.

He chewed and chewed, savoring the dish before at last swallowing. As the smell of the slightly fermented, spicy and lard-filled noodles before him tickled his nose, Jotun dove back in for more with a low growl, consuming and finishing the dish before him within seconds.

Good thing he had ordered three more.

FOUR
Lily's Return

"Like an animal," Eleanor sniffed, watching as Jotun finished his plate in record time. Even as she disparaged him, she had inched a little taller in her chair and leaned over unconsciously, licking her lips as she stared at the untouched plates.

"Agreed," Tobias said. He was still working through his own golden fried rice, carefully portioning each mouthful onto his spoon before slipping it into his mouth, chewing with deliberation and a precise twenty times before swallowing.

"I wonder when mine will arrive," Eleanor muttered, looking over to the kitchen. She knew Mo Meng would do his best to ensure she had her meal soon enough. One of the characteristics of the restaurant was a preference for quick-to-cook dishes, what with the lack of additional hands. Rather than serving dishes that required significant handling during the cooking process, the majority of meals were set up such that each dish only took a few minutes to cook.

However, when you had customers who ordered multiple dishes at a time, it did slow down the process a little. Eyeing the other two regulars, Eleanor let out a sigh before her gaze snapped suddenly to the doorway. She almost rose in her chair before hesitating.

Eleanor was not the only one, for both the Clan Leader and Tobias had stopped, the shorter man going so far as to swallow early. His hands dropped beneath the table, resting on his belt and the tool pouches he carried, eyes narrowing under bushy eyebrows.

Sensing the change, Kelly looked up from where she had just finished writing down the latest order, for a pair of diners who had more eyes for each other than the strange atmosphere in the restaurant. Even Mo Meng paused for a fraction of a second, before his hands started moving again.

"She is a guest, just like the rest of you," Mo Meng called out.

The trio relaxed a little, only to tense again as the door slammed open. Sauntering right in without a care in the world, Lily arrived with a gust of wind; the noise of heavy falling rain preceding her entry. She was soaked to the skin, unlike her companion who held an umbrella.

Through narrowed eyes, Eleanor noted that the umbrella was not the only reason why the second entrant was dry. The younger man wielded magic superbly, barely an iota of magical energy leaking from him as he kept up a warding spell against the rain.

Umbrella closed, he leaned into the door to shut it, muttering about sudden rainstorms arriving out of nowhere. Toronto simply was not known for sudden rainstorms, certainly not the thunderstorms that seemed to have crept up on them.

Then again, Toronto was not known either for the presence of a highly magical jinn. So, it was obviously a day for firsts.

"No need to frown so much. I'm just another customer here, right, old man?" Lily said, startling Eleanor as she almost seemed to appear right in front of her. The woman hissed, surprised that she had gotten lost in her thoughts at a time like this.

Or perhaps not surprised, for she could sense the magic emanating from the jinn. Magic like fine wine, drowning Eleanor in it. Clamping down on her own instincts to draw deep, Eleanor smiled tightly in return, only for surprise to make her control relax as Mo Meng, without missing a beat in his cooking, replied.

"Look who's calling old. I'm a spring chicken compared to you."

The young man, following—and Eleanor knew who that was, for the jinn's companion was as infamous as she was these days—bowed a little to her as he came up to her table. "I'm sorry for bothering you. We'll find another table as soon as ummm...." He tilted his head to Kelly who had glided over, the waitress giving Lily a professional, if strained smile. "Hi. Table for two?"

"This way," Kelly said, gesturing to a nearby table. "We do try to let our guests have their privacy in here."

"Oh, but I don't think...hmmm..." Eleanor felt the flare of magic run through her, washing over her, before Lily continued. "Eleanor minds. Does she?"

"I..." Eleanor said, swallowing around the sudden dryness in her throat and the expression in Lily's gaze. An all too knowing, judging gaze. "This..."

"Lily!" A sharp call from the kitchen. "Also, Kelly. Order up."

"You're no fun..." Pouting, Lily stood, drifting over to the table where Henry was already waiting, shifting from foot to foot.

When Eleanor managed to look over, he mouthed an apology to her.

Somehow, that was the most amusing thing of all. The way the boy seemed to think he should apologize for the jinn. Then again, the fact that no one could control her was his fault, so perhaps it all balanced out.

"Sorry for the wait," Kelly chirped, arriving with the bowl of laksa and placing the dish down beside Eleanor. She found and placed a pair of chopsticks and a spoon for her use a moment later, made sure everything was suited before disappearing around the corner.

At that point, all thought about the jinn and her companion—the archmage in training—was cast aside. For there were more important matters before her. Much more than the fate of the world. After all, dinner was here.

"Not a lot of people in here," Henry remarked, having already made a decision about what he wanted to eat after glancing at the menu. Instead, he was paying attention to the surroundings, tasting the magic in the air and eyeing the trio of supernaturals.

Their glamour was of little use against him. After all this time, Lily had trained him how to see past the majority of common and uncommon glamours on an ongoing basis. It took only a little more effort to pierce the rarer kinds—the type that all three in this building wielded.

More surprising, in a way, for such an out-of-place restaurant, that there were mundanes in here too. A couple had preceded their entrance, taking a seat towards the back of the building so that they had some privacy. While the supernatural and the mundanes lived together on an ongoing basis, it was often because the mundanes were unwitting participants in the mixing. In a restaurant like this, without a sign, in a side street in the middle of downtown Toronto, he would have expected none to appear.

Yet, there they were. Sitting quietly, two of them mooning over one another, the third entirely focused on the dish before him. This restaurant was truly perplexing.

"I doubt Mo Meng wants a large crowd," Lily said. "The wards do a good job of keeping too many away. But it'll also always keep him busy."

"The wards?" Henry said, surprised.

"Attracting and repelling ones." She gestured above, a trace of purple energy escaping her fingers to highlight hidden wards to his eyes. He committed the wards to memory, knowing he would likely be quizzed about them later.

More homework.

In retaliation, he could not help but point downwards. "You're still dripping."

"It's just water!" she pouted.

"That the waitress will have to clean up."

"I could…" Lily waggled her fingers.

"Mundanes."

"Fine…" She stood up and sauntered into the bathroom, where a surge of energy flowed outwards.

In the meantime, true to Henry's words, Kelly had arrived with a mop and was wiping down the floor before heading for the nearby doorway, depositing a set of warm, fluffy towels. If she heard Henry's apology as she hurried past, she had given little indication of it.

By the time Lily returned, all too soon, with a new set of dry clothing—a one-piece dress that clung to her figure with each movement—Kelly was finished and hurrying over to deposit more dishes for the trio along with the mundanes.

"What will you have?" Kelly said, plucking her pad out when she was done.

"Everything!" Lily said immediately.

"Another one of those…" Eleanor muttered under her breath.

"I'll just have the char kuey teow and the dessert, please," Henry said politely.

Kelly nodded amiably, checked about their drinks before she went to provide the slip of paper to Mo Meng and get their refreshments. In the meantime, Henry eyed Lily's clothing, the fabric of which still gave off a slight glow of energy.

Lowering his voice, he asked. "Did you just teleport that here or…?"

"What did I say about using magic? Always use the least amount for your goal. It's easier to just shift the material type than teleport it."

"Easier…right…" Henry said, doubtfully. He barely even started when magical sigils started appearing in his vision, reminiscent of his old system. Ever since that initial alteration, Lily had never released the link between them, allowing her to continue to project such images directly into his vision.

It made teaching him much easier, of course, even if she refused to inject information into his brain directly.

Lips moving a little as he read over the sigils and spell formula, he tracked the information in front of him, eyes glazed and shifting. It was this sight that Kelly, coming back with the drinks, returned to. Barely acknowledging her, Henry kept reading while she placed a pair of coconuts and a glass of soy bean milk before them.

Magic called, and Henry, once again, answered.

FIVE
Curry Laksa

In the kitchen, Mo Meng noted the actions of his customers but kept his attention on his task. He had another bowl of curry laksa to make, which was simple but still required a degree of attention to be paid. A good curry laksa was made from scratch, which meant that the laksa—the curried soup—portion had to be made beforehand.

The laksa consisted of two major parts—the broth and the laksa paste that was dissolved in the broth. To ensure a clean and clear taste that did not overwhelm with too much variety, Mo Meng preferred a chicken broth—sometimes, depending on what other scraps he had left around, mixed with a touch of prawns. However, the majority of the broth—a simple, clear and clean bone broth rather than western broths—was made in large batches by Mo Meng days earlier and then stored in the freezer.

Good broth had to be made by boiling chicken feet, neck bones and other bone parts from the bird over a period of twenty-four hours. The addition of a minor amount of meat and a lot of skin and fat ensured that the broth was rich and filled with umami. When possible—like today—additional prawn skins were added to the broth, layering it with a clean, mild seafood flavor.

Once the broth was ready, the scum skimmed away, and the broth itself strained, the laksa paste would be added and mixed in thoroughly. Like the broth, the paste was made beforehand and could be refrigerated for future use, since the mixture of spices and chili kept it fresh. In fact, the slow marrying of flavors improved and reduced the bite of the curry paste.

Laksa paste was made from a combination of shrimp paste—pre-toasted in a pan—blended with additional dried shrimp, dried and fresh chilies, galangal— a ginger variant with a more citrusy flavor that gave it a peppery, spicy bite with a touch of zest and pine — candlenuts, turmeric, garlic, shallots—not onions, for the shallots were sweeter and less sharp— lemongrass and chili peppers. Mo Meng's own version also added star anise—the fragrant spice giving the laksa an additional oomph when added—and some cumin for the color and taste.

For today, Mo Meng had taken the shrimp paste portions for tonight's dinner out early, letting it warm till it hit room temperature before frying it at low heat in a frying pan. Once the fragrances from the spices had been fully unlocked, he added the laksa paste directly to the broth that had begun simmering on the side, stirring the mixture thoroughly till it was fully blended.

Once the pot of laksa was boiling well, coconut milk—santan, in common Malaysian parlance — was added to it. Unlike coconut juice, coconut milk was derived from grinding the meat of old coconuts and squeezing the juices from the ground coconut meat. Though younger coconut meat could be used, it was the older, shriveled coconuts that gave the best flavor and strength to the dish.

Of course, using santan was tricky, since it mellowed the flavor significantly and smoothed out the dish. Too much and it would overwhelm the spices, so as he poured it into the broth, Mo Meng made sure to taste the concoction to achieve a proper blend of warmth, spice and fragrance.

Once that was done, the base curry broth was ready. Cooking the remainder of the meal was a matter of adding other pre-cooked ingredients to the dish, and the kind and variations varied by chef.

While musing on the variety of laksa toppings he had experienced, Mo Meng stirred the pot of laksa once more before grabbing a handful of thin rice vermicelli—beehoon—to throw into a waiting strainer ladle. Dipping the ladleful of noodles into a pot of furiously boiling water, he picked up a pair of long chopsticks, swirling the beehoon around to ensure it did not stick. Within a few minutes, the beehoon was cooked through, the thin noodles not requiring much time. Then that was placed in an empty bowl before additional toppings were added.

In Mo Meng's case, that meant shredded boiled chicken meat—broth from the boiling to be used in the future to make chicken rice—pre-cooked tofu puffs, bean sprouts and shrimp. A ladle of piping hot laksa water was drawn from the pot and poured carefully over the entire bowl, warming the meat and other toppings before the final touches were added. A lightly cooked egg, split in half, was added and then, in a separate spoonful, blood cockles.

Just like that, the dish was finished.

"Orders up!" Mo Meng called, placing the dish on the sill before turning to the next ticket. Even from here, he could smell the fragrant coconut curry filling the surroundings, mixing with the fried char kuey teow and the occasional groan of pleasure from his customers, and he smiled.

This was what made life worth living.

The bowl of curry laksa was brought swiftly, along with a plate of golden fried rice, to the young couple. The young lady, dressed in a purple romper, smiled in gratitude when Kelly placed her rice before her, while the man brightened even further as the laksa was served to him. After checking, Kelly swept away to bus some plates back into the kitchen, leaving the pair to their meal.

"It smells amazing. And it's Malaysian food. You have no idea how long it's been since I had some," Desiree gushed to her date. "How did you find this place again?"

"Oh, well…" Ashton paused, rubbing his nose in thought. "I…well, I…" Frowning heavily, he tried to remember how he had heard of the place. "Maybe a food blogger? No. I didn't read it. Maybe a video?" Now he was sweating, the smell of the chili rising up to brush at his nose even as he tried to remember.

"Well, I'm liking this foodie part of you." Eyes gleaming with humor and desire, Desiree picked up her cutlery. She scooped up a spoonful of fresh grains and slipped it into her mouth, chewing gently on the dish, feeling each individual grain as it melted in her mouth, and let out a rather inappropriate moan.

Not that the rest of the regulars paid much attention to her. Though both Henry and Ashton blushed a little, one from embarrassment, the other from future visions the noise conjured up.

Only when she had swallowed the mouthful did Desiree cover her mouth, blushing a fetching pink when she realized the look her date was giving her. "I'm sorry. I…it's really good!"

"Of course. It's fine, it's fine," Ashton said, already making plans to look up additional restaurant listings. He might have had a mild interest in food before, but he certainly had a large interest in the young lady before him. In fact…

Shaking his head, he dismissed the thought. It was only the third date.

"Aren't you going to eat?" she asked, bringing his attention back to his own bowl. And the rather ravenous way she was looking at it.

"Oh, yes. Do you want to try mine first?" he offered.

"No. Well, yes. But only after you've tried it! It's rude for me to have it before you."

"Oh, right."

"So eat up!" She waved her spoon at him, pushing him to try his meal.

He laughed a little at her antics, even as he picked up the chopsticks and spoon that had been placed at his side of the table. He shifted the chopsticks a little in his hand, not being entirely comfortable with the utensils, before debating what to do. Catching her impatient gaze, he shrugged and dipped spoon and chopsticks into the brightly colored, red and yellow dish.

A part of him wondered how hot it really was. The sambal that had been delivered in a small plate on the side indicated it could go even spicier, but best to test before adding any further spice. How embarrassing would it be to have his meal be too spicy to eat?

On the other hand, they did say spice increased the libido…

The first spoonful he withdrew from the curry bowl was a mixed one, filled with the white, slightly yellow-stained noodles, bean sprouts and a piece of chicken. Lifting the entire thing up, with the laksa sauce filling the rest of his spoon, he bent over his dish and bit down onto it all, slurping a little to get around the heat and the long noodles.

Beehoon—the rice vermicelli noodles—were thin and perfectly cooked, just a tiny bit of chewiness left in them to give a satisfying bite, but not undercooked so that it was hard or brittle to eat. The noodles had soaked in the curry laksa long enough to pick up some of the taste of the curry itself, without being in it so long that it had sucked the bowl dry or become overpowering.

The curry laksa was a delicious mixture of aromatic curry spices, chili, fragrant prawn paste and lemongrass, along with the velvety, rich smoothness of the santan. Mixed in the strong, well-cooked chicken and prawn broth, the laksa brought out high degrees of heat, spice and umami that had the man breathing through his mouth; but also chewing quickly to swallow down the meal.

The crunch of bean sprouts in his mouth, the village chicken, lightly boiled and soft, without any hint of gaminess, tender to the mouth and filled with flavor in each bite. It gave the noodle dish, with its strong curry flavor, a different, lighter texture and allowed Ashton to chew the mouthful a few more times before swallowing the entire dish down, feeling the heat of the laksa slide down his throat.

Relieving the spice with a little 'aaah' of pleasure, Ashton blinked when he realized that his date was staring at him fiercely from across the table. Even before he could excuse his behaviour, she was reaching across the table with grabby hands.

"Let me taste!"

Almost reluctantly, the man scooped up a spoonful for the impatient woman, handing it over with a mournful expression. Caught up in his sacrifice, neither he nor his date heard the comment from Tobias, though the rest of the room did.

"Ah, true love it is then, to allow another a mouthful of Meng's cooking."

SIX
Newcomers

The sound of rain coming down hard washed over the restaurant once again, as the door was swung open. A trio of newcomers stepped in, two men and a woman dressed in severe charcoal-grey and black suits and a pantsuit. They shook the rain off their bodies, none of the trio having an umbrella to share between them and all of them looking deeply unhappy. When they spotted the towels piled beside the entrance, the man who had first entered and the woman nearly leapt for them, colliding a little as they did so. The final entrant, a little younger than the other two, struggled to close the door against the harsh winds blowing outside before it slammed shut, startling the customers within.

"Apologies. The door…" He trailed off, gaze drifting to where Henry and Lily sat. Of the entire restaurant, only Lily was not paying attention to the entrants, her studious focus on the meal before her a marked distinction.

"I'm sorry." Kelly hurried over, looking at the door with a frown. "I'll make sure to oil the hinges later. It never gets stuck like that."

Henry shook his head a little, turning away from the newcomers to whisper to Lily. "That was you, wasn't it? The door. And the rain that cut through their weather enchantments." No answer from Lily, but he could see the glint of humor in her eyes. "You're a child."

"And they can't take hints," Lily said, setting down the soupspoon of curry laksa in the bowl. "I didn't want to be interrupted while eating."

"You could have…" He trailed off, shaking his head. "Well, not without breaking the limits that you've set yourself."

"Exactly. What do I say?"

"Too much magic is as bad as too little," he replied by rote. "So calling a magical storm that doesn't appear normally and making it soak them isn't too much magic?"

She nodded firmly, and when he frowned; she grinned. "It's all in how you do it. The storm was coming anyway. I just made it come a little faster. It'll change the natural flow a little, but I already planned for that. Means there's going to be a big mass of plastic washing ashore on an island in the Philippine archipelago in a few months, though."

By this point, Henry knew exactly what she meant and sighed. "I guess I should be buying a bunch of plastic bags, eh?"

"You can work on your summoning skills, too. Sand makes the worst golems, which makes it great training," Lily replied. Having said her piece, she went back to consuming her laksa, while Henry watched the trio dry themselves off as best they could before taking a seat near the entrance.

It put them a good few tables away, but close enough that he could read their auras and their magical pulse.

Now that Lily wasn't actively cracking their shielding spell, it had returned to force, layering each of the mages—and they were Council Mages—with a low-level defensive spell. Unlike his own Force Shield when he started, it was a reactive shielding bubble; meant to trigger additional spell wards when something hostile crossed the initial barrier.

It was quite fascinating to stare at, as were the low-level drying spells the trio were using. Each of them was using a different spell, meant to help dry themselves surreptitiously. The youngest was a water elemental mage, and he was wicking the water away into a small reservoir that was located in...

"His shoe?" Henry muttered, getting a slight nod from Lily.

Weird. But useful to store extra water when you were an elemental mage, he assumed. The woman was taking a more direct route, heating her clothing and herself so that, if you paid close attention, you could see the steam rising off her.

And the final man's magic was...he was...

"If you keep staring at him, someone will think you're smitten," Lily's voice cut through his concentration, causing Henry to jerk.

"I'm not...his magic..."

"Spatial. He's teleporting the water away, bit by bit." To Henry's surprise, there was a trace of respect in Lily's voice.

"Just the water?" Henry said, surprised. "The control that would take..."

"Is staggering. He's a prodigy for certain," Lily confirmed.

Henry tried to imagine what it would take, to cast magic so close to the skin, to teleport it away and do so for something as active as water. While it was a great medium to cast spells through—being able to take in magic with ease—that usually required the water to be still. Sitting and talking as he was, his body breathing, the water dripping, it required extremely fine targeting.

"Is he a Master?" he said.

"Archmage at least." She shrugged. "No surprise. They wouldn't send anyone less here, after all."

"After all?" Henry's eyes narrowed. "What aren't you telling me?"

"Lots!" Lily leaned in. "But you want to know something important?" At his nod, she pointed a finger down at his meal. "It's getting cold."

Growling a little under his breath, Henry dug into his meal. He knew when she got into a mood like this, she was not going to answer him. Not until she decided it was time. All he could do was wait. And maybe check on his own shield focuses.

Just in case.

"I told you that storm was magical," the younger man complained, glaring at the other two even as he continued to wick the water away. Not that being wet was too uncomfortable for him, but his wool suit was not the kind that would take being dried in that way that well.

"Amir, we did not disagree that the *woman* made it. We were arguing about the level of magical density used to enact such a widespread weather spell," the woman said. "Even when she was wielding it against us, I could barely sense the Mana in use."

"That is because, Marilyn, the initial locus point was much further away, as I have stated multiple times," the last member of the group muttered, his fingers weaving a gentle bubble of air around them that their words bounced off repeatedly, so that none of the mundanes could hear them.

"It should still have had a much higher ratio of Mana than what we experienced," Marilyn said.

"Only with the systems the Council uses," Amir said. "It's why we're tracking her, isn't it? The things she knows…."

"And can do," Archmage Wolfram finished. "She is a danger, but also a useful tool."

"Not nice to call me a tool." Lily's voice projected into their bubble, even as she continued to chew in silence over by Henry's table. "In fact, that kind of thinking is the kind that makes me a little…testy."

"And calling down a tropical storm isn't you being testy?" Amir said, only looking a little startled. After the third time she had shown an ability to pierce their toughest privacy wards and chose to speak with them, surprise was a hard emotion to conjure.

"Nope." Then, silence, as the group waited to see if she would answer further.

"I really hate it when she does that," Marilyn said, giving the pair a deathly glare.

"We do need to apologize. After all, we're here to—" Archmage Wolfram cut his words short, his fingers twitching once harshly as he cut the flow of Mana to the bubble, as Kelly walked over with three glasses of water.

"Welcome. I'm glad you found the towels, and you're all looking much better already. Can I get you a drink before you start?" Kelly said cheerfully, as she set the water down.

"Umm…coconut water, please," Amir said.

Marilyn, on the other hand, cast a dismissive look at the board, before she shook her head. "I'll stick to water. Also, do you have any proper food?"

"Marilyn!" Amir cried out, shocked.

"Proper food?" Kelly said, a little puzzled, with the same professionally nice smile on her face. "I'm not sure what you mean. Tonight, we're serving food from Malaysia. Our restaurant does theme nights, and tonight, well, it's southeast Asian cuisine. If it does not suit you, I'm sorry to say we don't have anything else."

"It'll be fine," Wolfram said, offering Kelly a smile and glaring at Marilyn. "It all looks—and smells—delicious. Maybe coconut water for us all, and ummm…what is this char kuey teow?"

"It's a fried noodle dish. Quite luxurious, a little charry and soy-sauce flavored. Very rich." She looked over at the older man, with his thinning blond hair and slight paunch, and added, "Perhaps the golden fried rice for you and the lady?"

"I'd like the curry laksa," Amir butted in. "I haven't had good curry laksa in ages."

"Oh, you've eaten it before?" Kelly said, smiling.

"I have. Visited Singapore in my teens," Amir said.

"Ah, this is Malaysian curry laksa, not Singaporean. More concentrated, less coconut."

"I'm sure it'll be good."

She nodded, looking at Wolfram who, touching his paunch which she'd noticed, added, "I'll have both the rice and the char kuey teow."

"If there's nothing else…I guess rice can't be too disagreeable," Marilyn said.

Still smiling, Kelly repeated the orders before spinning on her heel and leaving the group behind. The moment the waitress had left, the Archmage popped up the spatial bubble again, a furious but silent argument erupting behind it.

SEVEN
A Quiet Night

"We got another one," Kelly said to Mo Meng as she dropped the order ticket over the counter. Her lips were compressed a little, displeasure showing on her face now that she was no longer facing the customers. Couldn't let them see how annoyed she was.

Not that Mo Meng would have said anything if she had said something. While he might not get very angry from insults to his cooking, he was a good boss too, and didn't expect perfection from his employees. Just a willingness to let his strange customers live and bygones be bygones.

"Another ticket?" Mo Meng said, playing oblivious on purpose as he plucked the ticket from her hand and added it to his list. Not that it was a particularly busy night, what with the rainfall outside. That was enough to make him glare a little at the jinn, for he disliked wasting food.

Well, it would not be a real waste, for he would ensure it was provided to the homeless and hungry. Still, he liked cooking for people in his restaurant, letting them partake of his dishes in a comfortable environment while it was still warm.

"Another Karen," Kelly said.

"Mmm." Mo Meng paused, considering. "That's the females who show themselves on the internet, right?"

"No, that's a thot. A Karen is a grumpy, domineering, middle-aged woman," she replied, shaking her head. "How can you remember all your recipes but not that?"

"You'd be surprised how many names come and go. Recipes don't change…" Mo Meng said. "Well, unless we change them, and even then, that's a matter of meeting changing tastes. Or reintroducing new ones."

Kelly watched as the man turned away to start on the coconuts. She scanned the room once again, taking the time to make sure that each guest had a chance to catch her eye. A hand was raised, the other mundane customer at the end looking for the bill as he made the small signing gesture that was all too universal.

Flicking a glance back towards Mo Meng, who was busy prepping the coconuts, she did a quick calculation and headed over to the counter, grabbing the machine and the bill. Holding both in hand, she arrived at the man's table. The stranger had a small, satisfied smile on his face.

"Was everything to your satisfaction, sir?" Kelly said, curiously. It was always interesting to hear what the guests had to say about the food, though Southeast Asian was nowhere as adventurous as some of the meals that Mo Meng liked to serve.

"Oh, very much so. It's amazing. I'm surprised that there's not more news about the restaurant. You don't even have a Yelp listing!" A shake of his head at that thought.

"You really should. And a Google Places and a Facebook page and a website. If you want, I can help with that." A hand dipped into a pocket and a card was proffered.

"Oh, that's very kind. I'll definitely let the owner know," Kelly said, taking the card. "And how will you be paying today?"

"Card."

He took the machine, flicking through the options for tipping before tapping the top with his card. Kelly looked away while he did so, verifying that Mo Meng had finished with the coconuts before thanking the man and watching him happily amble away. Carrying everything back including his empty plate, she deposited the dishes and the machine, slipping the receipt onto its spike and the card next to the pile of other offers.

That pile was getting quite high, and she'd have to clear it soon. Casting a glance at Mo Meng, she girded herself for that battle once more. Convincing her boss to actually publicize his restaurant was her Sisyphus labor.

But one day, she'd succeed!

Till then, it was a good thing he paid her a good wage, or else she'd starve.

Watching Kelly walk off with the three coconuts, her recommendations to publicize the restaurant once again ringing in his ears, Mo Meng shook off the thoughts and focused on his dishes. Char Kuey Teow to start, he decided, for the wok was warm and the noodles soaked.

Really, with the unnatural storm pounding above and the runes of attraction working overtime, it was unlikely he would receive any additional customers. Which was a pity, since he did enjoy playing with the woks. More importantly, practicing with the wok was important; or else he'd lose his familiarity and end up burning the dishes.

Quiet nights were all well and good when you had busy nights in between, evenings where the crowd was packed wall-to-wall and there was scarcely any standing room. But the restaurant never had those. Not in the last decade that he had created it in this location, not since Kelly had arrived.

Which, perhaps, was why she was so insistent that he actually do things like have a sign and 'drag himself into the twentieth century at least, if not the twenty-first'. Truth be told, the world had changed so fast in the last few decades, Mo Meng was finding himself a little lost.

It used to be that a simple restaurant, with a simple attraction and repelling ward, would eventually grow a decent clientele. Some mundanes, but more important for Mo Meng, a viable and regular supernatural clientele.

These days, though, the supernatural had started mingling with humanity ever more, with full-on government branches dedicated to keeping these supernatural denizens contained and their secrets hidden. For the few mundanes who managed to stumble onto the truth, there were counter-measures in place—from the simple disbelief of the public, to blackmail and discrediting.

In reality, many mundanes moved on, content to leave the supernatural to themselves. Ghost, wraiths, vampires—it mattered not, there was a scientific explanation for it all. And when there wasn't, more than one human enjoyed existing in a state of minor myth. It created a sense of wonder that was all too often lacking in this modern, sophisticated, technological world.

All of which was well and good—but it meant that the supernatural community, much like the mundane one, had fractured even further. Leaving people like Mo Meng, who had yet to catch up and without a guide like Lily's Henry, to flounder along.

Repeating past mistakes.

That was a rather sobering thought for Mo Meng. He knew all too well how dangerous it was, for one as long-lived as he—and other quasi-immortals—to become staid and stale. Not that he was a vampire that might get staked for staying too long in a seaside resort, or a ghul whose consumption of the local bodies at the crematorium might harness an angry village.

But he was still a member of present civilization, unlike some of the immortals and buddhas, the demi-gods and the Norse gods who had retreated into their realms above, locking themselves away rather than deal with a changing world and dwindling moments of worship.

Musing about his place in this new-fangled society, with twits and thots and Karens, Mo Meng finished plating the first dish and moved on to the golden fried rice. Best make sure it tasted good. And perhaps ensure a bottle of ketchup was available.

EIGHT
Coconut Water

Clan Leader Jotun pushed the plates aside, smiling up at Kelly as she came by to sweep his dishes away. He fished in his pocket, coming up with a golden credit card that he set on the table for later use, the card landing with a solid thunk.

Turning his head, the young mage accompanying that annoying jinn stared at him and the card, a deeply puzzled expression on his face. Really, it was strange why humans found it surprising. What kind of giant—and Chief of Giants at that—would he be if he did not arrange for his gold card to be actual gold? It had given the crafters some minor trouble, to replicate the actual card the organization had sent, but that was the advantage of being Chief.

Jotun tilted his head to the side, dismissing the young man. For all his expertise—and he expected the boy to have some decent amount of skill from the stories told of him—the jinn was of more concern. Not that he believed in her innate wickedness or villainy. His people had been tarred with that brush all too often—especially by those damnable Marvel movies.

It was a pity they had ignored the comics and other artistic industries in North America for too long to be able to influence their works. Even now, the investments they had made were not paying off to the extent that he had hoped. It would take time for the world to see another side of the frost giants.

Damn Odin and Thor and their blasted propaganda. Cowards as they were to run off to Valhalla, to leave Midgard when their worship was waning, they somehow managed to make the clan's lives miserable.

As he sighed a long, deep sigh, his gaze tracked over to another group that made everyone's lives miserable. Not the jinn— though her rain was less than convenient— but the trio that had arrived after her. The Mage Council, arbiters of magic in the supernatural; or so they considered themselves.

In truth, just one of many hidden powers vying for control and power. Attempting to keep themselves relevant in a world that grew increasingly complex by the day.

And now, here they were, following after the jinn like a pack of mangy dogs, hoping for the scraps that she might drop their way.

Or…

"They're not just looking for scraps this time." The voice cut through his consideration, making Jotun frown as Eleanor gracefully took a seat beside him. She had brought over her own cup, waving a little to Kelly when the waitress caught her eye to indicate her new location.

"More reason to leave," Jotun rumbled. "When Mages and powers clash, everyone else must watch for stray embers."

"All the more reason to stay," Eleanor said. "Otherwise, how will you know when it might explode?" Turning to point out the window, she continued. "Anyway, do you want to be out there right now? The storm is destroying glamours and penetrating mage shields without a care."

"I thought the boy said it was only them?" Jotun rumbled, grumpily.

"Mostly them. But the jinn's control is not as strong as she likes to think." Eleanor's chin lifted a little, her lips drawing into a tight smile. "She might have knowledge and strength, but too much time in her lamp has seen her actual skills degrade."

"Was it not a ring?" Jotun said.

Eleanor let out a long sigh, of one whose brilliance was once again missed by the general public. Jotun ignored it, though he chose to slip his solid gold card back into his pocket. If the magic out there really was wearing down glamours, he would do his best to avoid it.

And he had to admit, he was a little curious.

Coconut water—the drink of choice for hipsters and workout enthusiasts. And the occasional armchair survivalist whose understanding of medical terminology extended to urban myths and the occasional TV show.

No surprise, then, that Marilyn eyed the shaved coconut with some trepidation. She was a proper lady, not some young fool who insisted on building muscles like a man doing weightlifting and eschewing proper cardio exercises like water aerobics.

The cook—easily seen through the open window, and at least that meant she could see how spotless the kitchen was or else she would never have even dared touch something from a place like this—had taken his machete to the coconut, lopping off the sides and shaving off the top with a few practiced strokes. Now the top could be easily seen, a metal straw sticking out of it and a small teaspoon set beside the plate.

A metal straw. What happened to good old plastic? "Are they trying to chip my teeth? You know I'll sue if they do…" Marilyn muttered, eyeing the straw with concern.

"It's probably for the environment," Amir said. "You can rewash the straws."

"And get inside properly?" Marilyn pulled a disgusted face.

"There are small brushes that go into the straws." Moving his hand over the entire display, he leaned back after a moment in satisfaction. "It's clear. No poisons, nothing of concern. Cleaner, actually, than most places we eat at."

"Perhaps where you eat…" Marilyn sniffed.

Amir bit his lip, not wanting to point out that the results from some of the 'posh' places that Marilyn enjoyed visiting had often come back even worse. Just because a place looked like it was clean, with bright lights and new designs, said little about the kitchen within.

Unlike this location. Which was scarily clean. In fact, they could have eaten straight off the table. A thought that had the man staring at the table itself, consideringly.

"Well, I guess one must make do. I am parched," Marilyn said, before slipping the metal straw between her cherry-red lips with care. She pursed her lips so that the straw would not touch her teeth, and sucked on the coconut.

Coconut water was, naturally, extremely mild in taste. There was the slight tingle from the electrolytes that were part of the coconut, a tiny bit of saltiness and sweet with an aftertaste of nuttiness. The drink was rather refreshing, and now that Marilyn had dried off, invigorating.

Sipping on the drink more contemplatively, Marilyn was reminded of a case in the sixties that had dragged her to Thailand. An annoying rogue mage who had used his magic to create counterfeit bills, in such quantity that the Mage Council had to step in.

Her first real case, and when she had finally caught him after staking out his residence for days on end along a deserted beach, she had seen fit to take small break. Away from the prying eyes of the Council and her husband, she had spent a week lying in the sun, soaking up the rays and indulging herself with some of the ladyboys that had thronged the streets of the nearby town.

Not that she would ever tell anyone any of that. In fact, that moment of risk was a dark secret, one she had locked away a long time ago. Yet the coconut water, so common back there and then, reminded her of that time, when she had been a little more…open.

Without prompting, she let the straw fall from her lips and picked up the spoon. Spearing the soft, almost translucent flesh of the young coconut, she peeled it off by scraping the sides and lifted it to her lips.

The translucent, whisper-soft flesh slid into her throat, touching her lips like the light kisses Lamai used to place, and then it was in her mouth and down her throat. Slipping in, like evening promises.

Broken promises.

Blinking, Marilyn leaned back, returning to the present as she set the teaspoon down. She dabbed at her lips lightly, casting a glance around. Amir had missed it all; the young man was engrossed in his own drink, his fingers playing across the screen of a smartphone he had extracted.

As for the Archmage, the leader of this diplomatic mission…

He just smiled and nodded down at the coconut.

"Good, isn't it?"

And Marilyn found herself having to admit, it truly was.

NINE
The Missing Third

Henry was done, the meal before him finished. He waited, a little impatiently now, for his dessert. After all he had eaten, the fact that the dessert was coming out of that kitchen would have made him impatient enough normally. However, it was the presence of those three that really made him antsy to be done.

"You can stop glaring at them, you know," Lily said quietly, leaning her head on her hand. "They aren't here to do anything. And if they were, you wouldn't have to deal with them."

"You never know…" Henry said, darkly. "Not as though seemingly reasonable people haven't chosen to act like complete bastards before, right?"

Lily sniffed. "If you're talking about Marrakesh…"

"I am."

"I have history there. I told you."

"No, actually, you haven't. You've quite deliberately not told me the details of whatever history you have there. Even though I've asked," Henry said. "Nor have you discussed other jinn, the number of actual trapped individuals in such magical traps."

"That's because you might choose to free them!" Lily said.

"Exactly!"

"Just because you don't think it's right to imprison people forever—and I'll admit, that worked out well for me—doesn't mean it's not the correct course of action sometimes. You keep trying to judge the supernatural with human sensibilities—or twenty-first century sensibilities — and it's going to get you into trouble."

"And you think I should change, just because some of the people around there—the people with power in particular—are old fuddy-duddies who refuse to enter the modern era. Or hell, the Industrial one." Henry sniffed. "Just because they have power doesn't mean they still get to lord it over others."

"Exactly! But if you release those who haven't had a chance to change, or who don't want to change; you can't expect a good outcome."

Henry's lips thinned, shaking his head. "But what then? Leave them trapped for all eternity? You know how that felt more than me."

"Some of them deserve it," Lily said, crossing her arms. "Or do you want to release someone like Zipacna, who'd start up volcanoes and burn down cities just for fun? And then eat the half-cooked flesh of the survivors?"

"No. But there are others, who might have changed like you. Shouldn't they be given a chance?" Henry said. "It's not fair."

"Life's not fair."

"Exactly!" Henry said. "We can at least try to fix it. Or what's the point of all this magic?"

"You know, all your white-knighting, healing people in hospitals, has been a strain on our resources. You and the ex-Squire don't make our jobs easy," Amir interjected, projecting his voice over via a simple spell. "At the least, you could cast some glamours so they don't recognize or remember you!"

"Pretty sure Alexandria doesn't want to be forgotten," Henry said.

The third member of their tiny trio had been left behind on Lily's latest jaunt, having chosen to spend some time in the local hospice in Chile where they had been last, using her own brand of ability to deal with some lingering issues with supernaturals. While Henry had been helping, they both knew that one of them had to keep an eye on Lily.

"Her! She's as much a problem as you two," Amir hissed. "But at least she's not our problem."

"What do you mean, problem?" Henry's voice dropped low, growing dangerous. A hand on his arm made him blink, as the jinn shook her head. Reminding him, that for all his hard-earned skill, he was still a neophyte. The three Mages sent here were not just any old mages, but mages of the Second Circle at least, with the Archmage being in the first.

And though Henry might not care about the council's standards, he understood them well enough to understand that those here were not to be taken lightly. Or threatened.

"Sorry. But what do you mean?" he corrected himself, after a second.

Only to receive silence in return. When he looked back at Lily, the jinn offered him a small, sad smile.

"Alexandria knew you'd react like this. It's why we two came here," Lily said. When Henry tried to stand, she did not remove her hand from his arm, forcing him to half-crouch, half-stand awkwardly. "She has to come to terms with her old order herself. The Templars, her feelings about them and the way they train future knights. It's not your place to interfere."

"But I can at least support her!" Henry hissed.

"And you are. By trusting in her to sort it out."

Again, Henry tried to stand up but was forced to stay still by the iron grip on his arm. For all her slender figure, Lily was a creature of pure magic. Her physical form had no real truck with physics, beyond what she chose to allow.

"So was all this searching for Mo Meng just a scam?" Henry said, aggrieved. "Dragging me around for months across multiple continents."

"No. I really did want to find him," Lily said.

Henry stared at Lily and was surprised when she let him go, gesturing towards his seat. He hesitated for a time before finally choosing to sit, letting out a huff. "What's so special about him, anyway?"

"Why, he's a great cook!" Lily said, brightly.

"And I'm grateful to hear that."

Henry jumped a little, turning his head to stare at Mo Meng who had somehow appeared next to him.

Mo Meng stared at the tickets before him, eyeing the half-dozen requests for desserts. He looked outside, watching the customers he had, noticing that the pair of mundanes had chosen to leave after paying their bill. The other mundane was still working through his dinner, but he had no dessert on order. As for the others…

A quick review of their plates and their demeanour indicated they were not ready to finish their meal yet. Knowing that Kelly would let him know when it was required, he found himself banking the flames of his gas fireplace and pulling the wok off the stove. He chose not to wash it—not just yet. There might be more customers.

Though, sinking his senses into the magical runes surrounding the restaurant, Mo Meng could not help but think it unlikely. The magical storm above might be non-magical in its final execution, but the heavy rainstorm had a depressive effect on commerce anyway.

Especially for a place like his own, which relied upon the subtle urgings of magical runes built upon the theoretical underpinnings of a siren's call. Interlaced into the general noise of urban living, it pulled pedestrians from a half-dozen blocks around, drawing them closer, depending on the individual sensitivity to magic and their circumstances.

Mo Meng had to admit, he was rather proud of the runes. It had taken him over a year to fine-tune the process. And for years, the runes had worked well, drawing and sending away customers with alacrity. However, the last decade had seen its effectiveness fade; the siren call of smartphones and social media influencers drowning out the gentle beckoning of his magic.

Leaving only the supernatural to come.

And as much as Mo Meng enjoyed his supernatural customers, they were, as Kelly was wont to say—drama. Some of them were even rightly so titled with capital letters and multiple exclamation points.

Like Lily.

Making a choice, he exited the kitchen silently, listening to the heated conversation between apprentice and master before arriving at their table, choosing to interrupt only at the most opportune moment.

One thing Lily and he did agree upon.

It paid to make an entrance.

TEN
A Busy Night. Of Sorts.

"And I'm grateful to hear that," Mo Meng said to the pair. Henry startled, almost falling over before catching himself. He flushed a little before eventually taking a seat, eyeing the proprietor suspiciously.

At the same time, Lily sniffed. "You should be. And shouldn't you be cooking?"

"Not right now," Mo Meng said. "Unless you want your desserts?"

"Yes."

"No."

Apprentice and Master glared at one another, before Henry sighed and gave in. "No," he said.

"Well, in that case, I'm free to speak with my customers. Something I like to do sometimes." Taking a seat, Mo Meng sat with the pair, crossing long legs and leaning back as though he owned the place. Which he did. The restaurant, the building, the block.

Old age hath its privileges.

"And what do you talk about? You're such a scintillating conversationalist," Lily said, mockingly. Then, cocking her head to the side to see Henry, added more carefully. "Unless you've changed?"

"I have," Mo Meng replied. He flicked at an imaginary speck of dust on his white chef robes before continuing. "But mostly,

I listen. Most of my customers tell me what is truly bothering them.

"Sometimes, I can even help."

Lily snorted. Henry looked considering. And silence fell over the table, even as Kelly bustled around, helping the few customers there were. Including the Mage trio, who were staring at Mo Meng with ill-concealed distrust.

"So…" Henry coughed.

"Yes?" Mo Meng said.

"How much does your waitress know? Of, you know…" He gestured around.

"Her parents were killed by a rampaging troll," Mo Meng said, softly. "She knows enough."

Henry winced while Lily looked over at the bright Kelly with considering eyes. Trolls—which, in truth, was a bad term, since there were a half-dozen different species so named—were generally among the quieter types. It was why so many disparate groups, from the monsters that hid beneath bridges to half-human creatures living in deep, underwater caverns, were so named.

But they were all also powerful, and when roused to anger, difficult to put down.

"Good. Okay then. Right. So you overheard?" Henry said.

"That I'm a good cook? Yes."

"The other part," Henry said exasperated.

"Yes too."

"What do you think? Should I go help? I should, shouldn't I? She's helped me with all my problems. And I've had a lot of them, let me tell you."

"I'd rather you didn't."

"What…" Henry stopped, eyes narrowed. "I didn't mean it literally."

"I did."

"Is he always this infuriating?" Henry asked Lily.

"No." Lily grinned. "But he does like being the dominant one." Eyes glinting with humor, she leaned forward, arms crossed to push her bosom up suggestively. "Isn't that right, Ah Meng?"

"Don't give the boy the wrong idea. We never did anything like that," Mo Meng said.

Pouting, Lily gave up and slumped into her chair. "Bother."

Mo Meng's eyebrows twitched further, before he firmly turned away from the jinn to stare at Henry. "A man must follow his conscience at all times. Without a sense of honor, a man is nothing more than an animal, a creature of base desires and slovenly nature."

"Exactly! I should help her," Henry said, only to frown when Mo Meng raised a single finger.

"However, a man must also learn when to allow nature to take its course. A child cannot learn if it is never allowed to try. A soup is bland, if it only ever receives one seasoning," Mo Meng said. "Your friend is going through her own trial. One must learn to trust one's friends to weigh risk appropriately."

"And what if they've got a history of never asking till it's too late?" Henry said, glowering.

"Then, perhaps they need to learn."

Henry sighed, crossing his arms at not getting the answer he wanted.

Mo Meng turned to Lily next, arms idly crossed in front of him as he eyed the jinn. When she looked up and raised an eyebrow at him, he gestured to the trio of Mages.

"I didn't bring them!" Lily protested, to the unspoken question.

"Yet, here they are."

"Come on, they're just eating…"

"And do you intend to continue eating here?" he said.

"Of course."

Mo Meng tilted his head to the side where the corridor and door leading to the washrooms were. A slight exertion of his magical senses showed the new runes being carved inside the door and door frame, magic exerted with such subtlety that only he, the jinn, and Eleanor had noticed it. Flexing his own will, and sending out a tiny pulse of magic, he triggered a half-dozen runes embedded in the walls, shutting down the enchanting.

"Then stop dragging your problems into my restaurant. Deal with it," he said. "Preferably without causing a natural disaster."

Lily wrinkled her nose. "You've gotten boring."

"I've grown up. You might want to consider that," Mo Meng said.

For a second, the easy-going jinn disappeared as she straightened, dark eyes growing imperious. "You would not like a more serious, focused and 'grown-up' me."

Mo Meng felt cold sweat break out over his brow, his breathing tightening as the protective runes in his restaurant flexed, put under a great strain. The entire building shook a little, and Tobias, still working through his meal, growled a little and stamped his foot. The trembling stopped as the earth stilled, the man growling a little about unseasonable earthquakes.

The three mages in the corner all reached inside their clothing, gripping at wands and casting implements, while Eleanor and Jotun just eyed the table.

It was Henry, though, who reached out and poked Lily in the shoulder. When the first poke received no reaction, he poked her again, harder, till she reacted, the growing sense of doom stilling.

"What?"

"I haven't had dessert yet," he said. "Destroy the building after dessert."

She glared at him for a second, then broke out in a wide grin. The feeling of overwhelming pressure disappeared, the energy suffusing and rocking the bindings fading away. She pointed a finger at Mo Meng before saying, "He's right. Dessert! Death and destruction later."

"Much later," Henry added.

"Only if the dessert is bad." She nodded. "Or I don't get seconds."

Rolling his eyes, the young mage slumped backwards into his chair, only surreptitiously wiping at his brow when Lily was not paying attention to him, having gotten into an increasingly loud argument with Tobias about her localized earthquake.

Mo Meng, mouthing a *thank you* to the young mage, turned back to his kitchen. He was not, he told himself, hurrying back to make dessert because he was afraid of the jinn. No. He was doing so because a customer had asked for a meal.

That was definitely the reason, and not a fear of the powerful jinn destroying years of runic work just because she was low on blood sugar.

Tobias finished chewing on the plate of golden fried rice, the meal having grown a touch chilly since its delivery many minutes ago. Still, it was just as tasty as it had arrived, the rice a little chewier, the spices a little denser, the egg chillier and more subtle. But now it was all finished, and Tobias was searching for Kelly. There was dessert left, and if he was lucky, it would be served before more shenanigans happened.

That was the problem with the surface dwellers. He still thought of them as that, even after a hundred and thirty-four years on the surface. It was but a blink of time, really, after six hundred and eighty-nine years underground before that.

Drama all the time. It was because they were all so hasty all the time. Never took proper care to do a job properly. Digging, digging, digging new shafts without shoring up those they made before. Now, look at them, with the problems they'd caused.

Fracking. What cracked-pickaxe kind of mind came up with such ideas? Pouring water into the ground where it wasn't meant to go, just to break open land to get at oil to burn in the atmosphere and destroy the surface world.

Fools, every one of them.

Good thing the clans had been working hard to slow down, divert and even take over many of the drilling operations. Whether through their proxies as corporate shills or just slinging pickaxes and guiding machinery, they had kept the majority of their lands safe. And the few times when all their work failed...

Well, that was why you came to places like this. And made friends with jinn and Archmages and other surface dwellers who did things other ways.

"All finished?" Kelly said cheerfully as she arrived by his side.

"Done," Tobias said. "Dessert, please."

"Of course," Kelly said. "I'll let the kitchen know."

Tobias nodded over to the jinn and her companion. "Mo Meng seems to know her."

"An old friend, I think." Kelly shrugged. "Why? Want an introduction?"

He considered for a second, looking between the jinn and the three mages. Then he shook his head. "No, another time. I think they'll want to talk soon."

"Those three..." Kelly paused, then sighed. "It's a busy evening, isn't it?"

"In a way." Tobias looked around the empty place. "You'll be good, then?"

Kelly chuckled. "Not to worry. The boss pays me a good salary. Tips are just that, you know?"

"Good. Never understood the North American obsession with tipping," Tobias said.

She smiled agreeably, then knowing that there was no more to be said, dipped her head low and went to tell Mo Meng. As she did so, she stopped by the other tables, confirming if they wanted their desserts. No surprise that they all did, all but the three mages.

Who had, finally, stood up to speak with their target.

ELEVEN
The Scourge

"Why are you bothering me?" Lily said, staring at the three that had crowded around her table. "I haven't done anything. At least, nothing that would bring this about."

"That's the point," Marilyn said. "You haven't done anything. No good, no evil, nothing!"

"Isn't that what you wanted?" Lily said, puzzled.

"Some of us did," Amir murmured. "Some of us just want you to be neutral. That was the prevailing wisdom of the council."

"Until recently," Archmage Wolfram said. "Then the scourge began."

"Scourge?" Henry said, interrupting.

"The mortals call it a pandemic. A virus." Marilyn shook her head. "Fools. Do they think it'd mutate that fast, escape so many boundaries without magical help?"

"It's a magic plague." Lily waggled her fingers. "Not a plague made by magic. They happen once in a while."

"Not like this," Marilyn said.

"No, exactly like this," Lily corrected. "Just because you don't recall doesn't mean it hasn't happened before."

"You are correct," Wolfram cut in before the pair could start arguing. The jinn turned to the man now that he was talking to her, head cocked to the side. "But it has never been like this before. Never so many connections, never spread so fast. Magic doesn't work, because it just generates new variants. Our best mages, our best healers are playing catch-up at best."

"That's what magic plagues do," Lily said. "You don't solve magic plagues with more magic. You just survive them."

"And when they strip glamour and strength, what then?" Amir said. "Mages are getting ill and coming out weakened, losing their touch for magic or their strength. Knowledge that they had taken years to acquire, suddenly no longer at their fingertips. Magical senses, magical muscles—changed or atrophied away."

"Then, they adapt," Lily replied. "That's part of being human, isn't it?"

"As if you'd know anything about being human," Marilyn snapped.

That made Wolfram glare at his fellow mage, anger in his eyes at antagonizing the jinn. Yet Lily looked entirely unphased by the accusation, instead nodding along.

"You're right. And this sounds like a very human problem." She paused, scratching her nose and looking sideways at the other customers. "You're all affected by the virus, though, right?"

Silence at first greeted her words, as the other customers, eavesdropping as they might have been, were surprised to be spoken to.

It was Tobias who answered her first, the dwarf smiling grimly. "Aye. It robs one of taste and smell for the ores, if you get it bad. Nasty business, it is. Know a cousin who lost it all. Six months later, he still has to work doing *paperwork*."

"It causes no such loss among our people," rumbled Jotun. "To lose love and taste of food and drink, that is a tragedy." Then the ice giant sighed. "But it hollows the chest nonetheless. Kills our eldest and most vulnerable. Many are forced to leave their homes, unable to stand the cold any longer; driven to *warmer climes*."

"Wait, wait, wait." Kelly, coming back after giving the orders to Mo Meng and carrying a pitcher of water, slowed down. "Are you talking about the virus? THE virus?"

Nods all around.

"It's magical? And it's affecting everyone differently?" Kelly said, incredulously.

"Yes. Humans have it worse," Henry said, from his seat. He raised an empty cup, and Kelly filled it for him with the water as he continued. "You see, we're kind of the genetic mutts of the planet. Same reason why we can procreate," at her frowning, he added "—have children—"

"I know what it means."

"Sorry. Anyway, same reason we can procreate with most races, it's the same reason why we get all the side effects," Henry said.

"It's also why humans are the plague rats of the supernatural community," Eleanor said, eyes glinting with dark amusement. "What they get, they spread."

Henry just shrugged.

"And you can fix it?" Kelly said, fixing her gaze on Lily with sudden intensity. "You can just…snap your fingers and make it all go away?"

"It would take a little more than just snapping my fingers," Lily said, offended.

"But you can do it."

Lily hesitated, looking at Henry and then at the other customers, who looked fascinated. And finally, her gaze landed on the mages who were waiting for her answer. For her to lie or prevaricate. And she found herself answering, truthfully.

"Yes."

Inside the kitchen, Mo Meng worked. Not that the process of making sago with gula malacca was difficult. In fact, the process of creating the dessert was one of the simplest. Sago balls were something that even Mo Meng purchased in bulk, for the necessary process to make the tiny, quarter-grain-sized balls was best done by machine. Once one found a good, clean supplier; half the battle was done.

After that, cooking the tiny sago balls just required a very large pot of water set to a rolling boil and an untiring hand to stir the contents. Pearl-white when uncooked, the balls were thrown into the water and allowed to boil till they were entirely clear.

The entire trick of cooking sago was to make sure enough water and enough heat was present when one began. Too little water, and the balls would stick together, refusing to part and spoiling the cooking process. Too little heat and the water would not boil, allowing the balls to fall to the bottom of the pot and stick. With sufficient quantities of both, though, and a hand that kept stirring the tiny balls to ensure they did not clump and the heat penetrated all the way, one was golden.

Simple, easy, sufficient.

Ten to fifteen minutes of stirring, and the sago should be entirely clear. Strain the entire concoction and run it through cold water, to ensure that the sago would form and keep to their initial spherical shapes.

Pour the strained, cooled sago into containers and place in the refrigerator to set overnight. And you were done with the base.

Of course, sago by itself had very little taste. Salt thrown into the water might add the barest trace of the mineral, but it was insufficient. Which was why chefs in Asia had come up with additional toppings to impart further flavor.

Putting the container of sago on the plate, Mo Meng turned to finish up preparations for the rest of the dish.

Traditionally, as Mo Meng preferred to consume the dish, the recipe required only two further ingredients: coconut milk— chilled as well—and a syrup made from gula malacca. Coconut milk to add a richness to the dish that plain milk failed to provide, while also having the side benefit of not containing lactose. And gula malacca—which some desperate cooks would substitute brown sugar for—in syrup form to add a smoky sweetness to the dessert.

If anything, it was the gula malacca that made the traditional dessert unique. It was created from the sap of palm trees; the sucrose-rich sap was tapped by workers and collected in metal pails before being boiled down and the thick brown syrup cooled. Traditionally, the cooling was done in a bamboo mould, allowing the taste of the bamboo to impart itself to the dish as well.

Pulling the thick, blocky chunks of gula malacca from his pantry, Mo Meng moved over to the waiting pot, water and a pair of tied-off pandan leaves set to warm. He picked up a knife, shaving down the edges of the gula malacca with long, easy strokes. He could have broken it down by hand, so soft and crumbly the high-quality palm sugar was, but this was faster. It also allowed the shavings to mix with the water and pandan leaves, requiring less stirring by him.

Already, he could smell the deep smoky flavor that the gula malacca imparted to the pot as it boiled, mixing with the fragrant fresh pandan leaves. One could not add too much sugar, but considering the number—and type—of guests he had tonight, a little indulgence would not hurt.

So Mo Meng concentrated the syrup a little more, shaving in more of the sugar than he usually would, thickening the syrup before he set the block of sugar aside. Then, after ensuring the gula malacca was well combined, the pandan leaves fished out; he poured the concoction into the waiting serving pitchers.

Placing these two final ingredients in tiny serving pitchers of their own on the plate along with the glass container of sago, Mo Meng was done.

Sago with gula malacca—traditional style—served.

The best part, in Mo Meng's mind, was that this dessert was almost always edible by even the most sensitive of dieters. No gluten, no lactose, no preservatives. Just three ingredients—four, if one counted the pandan leaves.

And it still tasted divine.

Smacking the bell to indicate an order was up, he moved on to plate another two such dishes. Then, after making a face at bending to the times, Mo Meng turned to the more strenuous options. The non-traditional methods of creating a sago dessert.

TWELVE
Sago and Gula Malacca

Kelly blinked, the ring of the bell making her body move before her brain caught up. She was still shocked by Mo Meng's friend. She knew, oh did she know, that he was strange and yes, powerful. Ever since she'd walked into the restaurant so many years ago, she'd known he was different. But this woman…

Well, she took the cake. Or the sago, in this case.

Because the moment she arrived back at the table, carrying the desserts, the customer snatched it off the platter and dumped it in front of herself, long before Kelly had a chance to do so. Which she would say was impossible, considering the physical logistics of it, if Lily had not chosen to subtly alter spatial dimensions in the restaurant.

Kelly had no magic of her own. Not like so many of the restaurant customers. She had, however, spent enough time in here to grasp when others were using magic— subtly or not so subtly. Rather than worrying about it, she mostly just got on with her job.

But when someone like Lily talked about just snapping her fingers, making the world twist and change based off their own whims, it made her remember that this little restaurant in the middle of Toronto, an almost literal hole-in-the-wall, was not your usual dining establishment.

Nor were its customers your regular office drones.

"Are you going to explain it to them, or not?" Henry said, arms crossed with a very put-upon look on his face.

Now, that was another enigma. He looked to be all of twenty-five, if she had a good read on his age. Not very old at all, and the way he acted, she assumed he really was in his mid-twenties, if a more mature twenty-five than most. So why did she get the feeling he was the powerful jinn's minder?

Lily was ignoring them, pouring a very generous dollop of the gula malacca onto her plate, watching it with a smirk on her lips as it collected and dribbled around the tiny, clear balls of tapioca. Henry watched her do so for a few moments more, before he let out a huff and turned his attention to the waiting mages. Somehow, though, Kelly felt that he was speaking to her.

"When Lily said it was not that easy, she meant it." He waved a hand around, indicating the restaurant. "This place is a great example of unintended consequences of magic."

A low, warning growl appeared from inside the kitchen, but Henry ignored it. Perhaps not the smartest thing, since insulting the magician whose food you were eating was just asking for it.

Not from your average amateur, at least.

"I bet the owner just wanted to cook. Of course, cooking means having the right ingredients, the right utensils, the right skills. He has the skills, but keeping ingredients fresh, keeping the workplace set up…that is made easier with magic. So he added the first layer, just simple preservation rituals. Then, of course, since he's here, he added a ritual for safety and security. Maybe an alarm one, a light geas of safety to make sure guest rights are in play. Nothing major, right?"

Silence from the kitchen, so Henry continued. Kelly had her head cocked to the side, curious to see where he was going with this, learning more with each word about her employer.

"The moment he started invoking magic, though, altering the flow of energy in the world, he lit this place up to magical senses. Now, I bet he didn't want that to happen. So he needed to hide the magic use. And probably himself," Henry said. "Most magicians end up using so much magic, they become like beacons to the trained."

The way he was looking at the three Council Mages was rather telling. The Archmage just smirked; the other two looked a little taken aback. New information, perhaps? Or something they just never cared to worry about.

Even Kelly knew, Council Mages thought they were all that.

"And your point?" Amir could not help but snap.

"Unintended consequences and an ever-growing list of fixes," Henry said. "Like remodeling an old house, where you pull off the dirty old carpet to find that there are old moldy tiles beneath which you then take apart only to find that the basement floor has cracked and you need to put in new concrete, but as you get ready to do that…"

"Malcolm's dad!" Kelly cried, snapping her fingers.

Lily, dribbling coconut cream on her sago, snorted. She cocked her head at Kelly, eyes narrowing. "Aren't you a little young to have watched that?"

"Streaming. And memes." Kelly rolled her eyes.

"Meme comments aside," Henry said, waggling his fingers. "All this magic utilization is the same. One problem solved, another one crops up. You keep smacking it with magic cures, but it never ends."

"And you're saying that Lily's cure for the pandemic is the same," Archmage Wolfram said. "That the cure is as bad as entire lineages of magicians losing access to their birthright." A lip curled upwards, in a sneer. "Tell me, oh wondrous child, how?"

Henry opened his mouth to retort, then closed it after a moment. He frowned, and Kelly could not help but note how he tried to speak once and then again. Something held him back, as he stared at the intensely glowering older man towering over him.

"You can't, can you?" Wolfram said. "Because this pandemic is a curse, one that destroys our people."

"I can, I just…" Kelly caught the glance Henry shot to Lily, before he clamped his lips shut. Something there, something he wasn't willing to say. She had seen that, with less intensity, less hesitation, happen with Mo Meng when he was asked a question he could answer but would not.

Secrets. They could eat you alive, sometimes.

"It doesn't matter. Lady Lily won't do it anyway," Marilyn said coolly. "Is that not right, jinn?"

And then the group fell silent, turning to stare at the raven-haired jinn who was gently poking with a teaspoon at her food, never having taken a bite. Not yet, at least.

"Mmmm?" Lily looked up and then shrugged. "Oh, yes. No, I won't."

"And better we are for it," Tobias rumbled from his seat.

The group turned as one to stare at the bearded gentleman. He returned their gaze placidly, nodding over to where Eleanor sat with Jotun to encompass the pair in his next statement.

"We have seen what happens when magic—often human-applied magic—is wielded without care. It is good that the jinn has learned circumspection."

"Hey! Most of those A-spells weren't my fault!" Lily cried. "Ring of wishing, remember?"

"A-spells?" Kelly whispered as she leaned down to ask Henry.

"Apocalypse-level spells," he replied.

She blanched, and then jerked as another ring alerted her to more food to be picked up. She scurried away, even as the conversation continued behind her.

"Choice or not, the plagues you have caused, the droughts and the banishments, resound still through our peoples," Tobias said. "Unintended consequences, indeed."

"And intended." Eleanor's interjection was harsh, vicious.

Lily bowed her head, hands opening a little. Pain and regret flashed through her eyes as she remembered many of the instances they had mentioned. A plague cast upon an elven village, to drive them out of forests that had been desired by the mage. A weather spell, to relieve a country-wide drought—that had created a desert two countries over, because the regular rains had not come for nearly a decade afterwards.

"A spell, wielded properly, has few of these unintended consequences," Archmage Wolfram sniffed. "If there are any, it is a lack of planning and skill on the part of the caster."

For a second, the regular background noise from the kitchen stopped. It was the shortest of pauses, but Lily noticed it. And even as it started up again, she found herself smiling, brightly.

"Let's talk about how you envision such a spell, then," Lily said. She scooped up a spoonful of the sago, grabbing translucent pearls and white coconut milk, a touch of dark sugar at the bottom. "What was your plan?"

"Mine?" Archmage Wolfram hesitated, then raised his chin. "The Council believes a targeted decay spell, using the known magical signature of the virus, should be sufficient."

"A single spell, using the virus's magical signature?" Lily nodded, gesturing with her free hand. A sparkling spiderweb graph appeared, one that shifted and moved with each breath, colors varying at each graphed point. "This magical signature?"

"Uhh…yes?" Amir said, squinting. "Fascinating. How did you get that?"

"Elementary, my dear mage," Lily muttered. "But how about this one?" Another gesture, and a second graph appeared. Similar to the first, except for a few points which throbbed.

"That's…the same?" Then before she could be corrected, Marilyn shook her head. "No, it's different. A variant, then?"

"Yes. A variant."

"So, two spells. Or one that will encompass both variants," Archmage Wolfram said.

"Very well." Lily's fingers twitched again, more magical spiderwebs appearing, each of them subtly different. "How about these?"

"They're all variants?" Amir said, slowly and carefully.

Henry, sitting beside her, let out a low *ahhhh*. He seemed to have realized something, as he stared at the spiderwebs, though his gaze flicked from one the other.

"Some minor variation in the spell form, to take in changes. The Hernandez-Frederique Variant Theorem should suffice," Archmage Wolfram replied.

"Really?" Lily lips thinned. "It'd target…eighty-seven percent." As she spoke, a majority of the spiderwebs faded away.

"Then you'd suggest another?" the Archmage said.

Lily shrugged before looking at Henry, her eyes questioning.

"I mean, the Ritten-Lemar Chaos Proxy Formula is a little more robust for something like this, but I might want to cross it with a more robust selection and discarding formula. Maybe the Thompson-Astra Hunter Principle?" Henry said, hesitantly.

"Better." Lily flashed him a smile, gesturing again, and another nine-tenths disappeared. "That just leaves…those."

Six spiderwebs, floating in the air.

"Easy. Individually targeted decay spells," Wolfram said, smugly.

"And you're happy with that?"

Wolfram nodded.

"And another cataclysm occurs."

THIRTEEN
Another Cataclysm

"What do you mean?" Wolfram snapped.

"Well, you killed all of the viruses you targeted, of course." Lily gestured, and the spiderwebs faded away, leaving a dark grayness hanging over their heads. Now that her hand was free, she reached for the gula malacca once more, positioning it over the spoonful of sago. "Now what?"

"What do you mean, now what?"

As she poured the gula malacca onto the teaspoon, soaking the tiny balls of tapioca, they slowly grew dark, the sugar overflowing the spoon. Lily did not answer, continuing to pour till the coconut milk could no longer be seen and even the clear balls had fully darkened.

"Now what do you want to do with all the dead viruses?" She waggled her spoonful, before slipping it into her mouth and letting out a low moan of pleasure. More than a few of her watchers winced, feeling a sympathetic ache in their teeth at the sheer volume of sugar she had just consumed.

"They're dead. What do we care?"

"Many reasons. You've just polluted multiple bodies with dead viruses, with a mostly targeted spell. Those dead viruses have to go somewhere. Some bodies, some individuals will not be able to handle the sudden influx of deceased viruses in their bodies, leading to the spread of decay magic through them." Lily picked at her dessert, pulling up some of the tapioca balls that had lingered at the bottom of her meal. "Their bodies will never clear these viruses, leaving them stained."

She waggled her spoon, illustrating before taking a bite. She chewed and swallowed, the group silent as she continued. "Then you've got those individuals with natural resistance against external magic, who might still hold reservoirs of such viruses. Any spell that overrides their defenses would also leave them vulnerable."

Another mouthful of dessert, scooped up and swallowed.

"More die, for your targeting also included a large number of helpful viruses and bacteria. Some of which have been out-competing other viruses." Her free hand rose up, gestured, and a series of faded spellworks brightened a little from where they had been hiding. "Maybe, probably, another magical pandemic or two brews. Not now, of course.

"Or not likely. But in a dozen years? A score? Definitely."

Archmage Wolfram shook his head. "We can refine the formula further. Track those who are reservoirs and contain them, burn out the viruses individually."

"Of course. But you've also unleashed a worldwide spell." Lily scooped up another mouthful of her dessert, waving it before him. "We start here. In North America. Magical energy gathered, to release it."

Bite. Chew. Swallow.

"Then, the magic spreads, to the east. Europe next."

Bite. Chew. Swallow.

"Africa."

Bite.

"Asia."

Chew.

"Asia again."

Swallow.

"Australia."

Two-thirds of the dish gone.

"South America."

She paused, the next spoonful wobbling on her spoon. "But you can't create something from nothing. Magic always draws from something. Are you pulling from the environment? Then wards fail. Demons are released. Magical aids, faded.

"Or do you tap the other realms?"

She popped the spoonful into her mouth and pointed at the three regular guests.

"Which one will you pick from? The Ice Realm maybe? The Night Lands? Or the Underdark?" She shook her head. "You know how it stands. The ones that are barren have little enough magic to pull. Would you steal from them, then? Start another magical catastrophe there?"

"The Council has reserves," the Archmage said, stiffly.

"Ah. The reserves. The release of stored magic from magical instruments and storage devices. A spell powerful enough to affect the world, enough energy to do so and target multiple individuals…" Lily nodded. "And how do you put that genie back into the bottle?"

"Really?" Henry said, scandalized.

"I had to," Lily said, grinning unrepentantly.

"So bad. Like a dad joke," he grumbled.

"But sexier!"

"Nope." Henry shook his head. "Not going there."

"I'm sexier, right?" Lily turned her attention to Amir, who refused to meet her gaze, and then Kelly, Tobias and Jotun in turn.

"You're a six," Eleanor said, repressively.

"Not all of us use supernatural charm to get our men," Lily sniffed at the woman.

Eleanor just grinned. "If you're not trying, you're not trying."

"I don't think that's how it goes…" Kelly started and trailed off, choosing to not get involved as she backed off to return to mopping tables.

Tobias, his own dish of sago before him—one filled with tropical fruits, including the ubiquitous mango—gave her a firm nod. She ducked her head a little in thanks.

"We can build energy collection platforms. We already have…" The Archmage ground to a stop, his eyes widening. He cast a glance at the three customers, all of whom were looking quite interested in what he had been about to say. "It can be handled."

"Unintended consequences," Henry said, waggling his fingers. "How much magic are we doing here now? How much else will you continue to add to it? Magic is not always the answer."

"It's rarely the answer," Mo Meng called out from inside his kitchen. "Some things just have to be endured."

"Like warm rain on a sunny day," Amir muttered, wiping at his hair which had, fortunately, mostly dried by now.

"Or a magical plague. Because it might otherwise mutate, to affect other species. Or fight off a spell, having hidden its presence amongst the many others of its kind," Lily said, scraping the bottom of her bowl and waving the gloopy mess of gula malacca and coconut milk that had been at the bottom of it around. "Or else we add more mess to the world, and somehow hope to clear it up."

"If that's the case, what's the point of magic at all?" Kelly said, speaking up.

"What's the point of fire? Or electricity?" Henry said.

"Lots."

"Exactly."

Kelly paused, then shook her head. "Do you mages study at being enigmatic? Or is it just that using magic makes you obtuse?"

"I blame our teachers," Henry said, looking pointedly at Lily who grinned unrepentantly. She made big gimme motions to Kelly, who sighed and returned with the sago topped with fresh fruit.

Setting the dish down beside Lily, Kelly stepped away.

"And that's it? That's your answer. Use magic within prescribed limits, don't try to fix the world?" Kelly said, frowning.

"I've seen many mortals who have tried to better the world," Lily spoke up, softly. She touched a slice of mango, pushing it aside. "Dictators." Honeydew slices, next. "Tyrants." Mandarins, their skin peeled away. "Wise men." Slices of strawberry, small and wild and sweet. "Kings."

She picked through the fruits, pushing down to the pearls of sago below before scooping them all up, slices of fruit mixed together with the sago and coconut milk. Mouthful of sweetness and tartness, the light, creamy taste of coconut milk on her tongue.

Then Lily sighed.

"Fools, all of them. Change one event, forestall one calamity, another arises somewhere else. Forestall a crisis here, and it builds till it becomes a calamity there." She shook her head. "A kingdom is saved, and the people who would have taken it starve."

"Then we do nothing?" Kelly growled.

"No. We change things, but slowly. Magic eases the life we live, but it cannot—should not—be used to change the world at large. We raise and teach, pass on knowledge and wisdom; and take much care for when we must wield our spells." Lily closed her eyes. "Because there will come a time when such magic is needed. There are things that only magic can fix."

"Things?" Kelly said.

Before Lily could answer, Archmage Wolfram flicked his hand to the side. "There are things we do not speak of. Dangers that are not for mortal ears."

The waitress frowned at the answer, but Lily nodded.

"The Mage Council are foolish at times. But wise at others." She smiled tightly before plucking another spoonful of sago. "This is one such time."

"And our request is a foolish one?" the Archmage could not help but ask.

When Lily nodded, the man raised his head to stare at the darkened runes that hung around them. His lips thinned, as he considered what had been revealed, the depth of his own knowledge. The degree of strength that the jinn had showcased and was further rumored to have.

And he finally inclined his head in acceptance. When his fellow mages seemed about to object, he gave them a stern look. They acquiesced to his orders, the chains of hierarchy delivering obedience. If a sullen one in Marilyn's case.

"Well, that's it, then. I think it's time for more dessert, no?" Lily said brightly. Somehow, in the intervening period, the rest of her sago dish had disappeared, along with Henry's. A fact that had the apprentice mage glowering at his friend.

Kelly snorted and turned away as the bell rang, going off to serve the rest of the dishes. As she did so, Mo Meng exited the kitchen again, carrying a tray with him. One that was riotous with colors, from white to green to purple and red.

FOURTEEN
Kuih

D essert. There were many kinds of
desserts that Malaysia was known
for. The Nonya—the children of
Chinese immigrants and the local Malay
population—had originated many such
dishes, including kuih, the bite-sized snack
often made of glutinous rice. There were as
many types of kuih as there were clans who
made it to Malaysia. More. And all of them
simple in theory to make, excruciatingly

hard to create in practice. Like the best dishes, the trick was not in the recipe but in the making.

No surprise, then, that Mo Meng refused to place any of his creations on the menu. Even decades after learning the initial recipes, his skill had not crested to a point where he dared to take the step of offering the dish to another for money.

As a gift, on the other hand, he was willing to risk it.

"More dessert. Yes, I think we can do that," Mo Meng said, setting the tray of kuih down. "That is, if we aren't going to try to convince the most powerful jinn on Earth to cause another cataclysm." His gaze trekked over to Henry. "Or sneak out more secrets for mortals that do not need to know."

The Archmage lips pursed, head bowed low as he eyed the colorful desserts with some trepidation. His fingers hovered over the selection, twitching from one to another. There was one that had pinkish-red and white layers, one after the other. Another, nearby, was cylindrical, green with a sprinkling of desiccated, shredded coconut across it.

"Lapis Merah and Kuih Lenggang," Mo Meng supplied. "The first is layered rice flour with coconut milk inserted, and each layer cooked before the next is added. Takes hours, but it's slightly sweet and savory. Very traditional. The kuih lenggang is a Malaysian coconut crepe with grated desiccated coconut soaked in gula malacca as a filling. A popular child's treat."

The Archmage nodded, picking up the layered cake. He turned it from side to side as he eyed the multi-layered dessert. "The Council will be unhappy with our results. They fear the damage to their families, the uncertainty of when the virus will attack, who it will affect. Our magic, their position, it is no safeguard against this pandemic."

"Though it can reduce their danger and increase their chances of survival," Amir muttered under his breath.

Marilyn flicked a glance over to the man, hurt flashing in her eyes. Still, his words were true enough that she chose not to argue. At least, not in public.

"But I shall assure the Council that the jinn will not be swayed." He tilted his head to Lily and added. "It will reassure some of the more militant members who have believed your presence, unconstrained, continues to be a threat. Restraint might be best for you, in the long term."

Lily offered a small smile at that, though she did not answer the unspoken accusation. Or clarify her reasoning further.

"Good. Then eat up," Mo Meng said, waving his hand down at the tray of kuih He pointed first to a half-dozen pandan leaf wrapped pieces, a glistening white topping on them. "The kuih pelita is a personal favorite. It's not there yet, but if I do say so myself, it's pretty decent," moving on, he pointed over to another white and green layered set, "while the serimuka is made of steamed rice flour and a custardy, mung bean variant pandan flavoring. I had to use processed pandan leaves for that, though, so it's not entirely what I would call my best work."

"So modest," Lily said, picking up the serimuka with her fingers and watching the top wobble a little. The green, custardy top shifted as she turned it from side to side, a small smile dancing on her lips. "I'm sure it'll be fine." So saying, she took a bite, letting out a little delighted moan as the salty, savory dessert mixed in her mouth.

"I will not say no to a free dessert," Eleanor said, sauntering over and picking up one of the lapis merah, a smile dancing on her lips too. "But I shall take my leave, too. Before some—" her eyes darted over to Marilyn and Amir as she spoke, "get further ideas."

"They would not," Mo Meng said, a hint of warning in his voice.

"I am sure. But there is no reason to slather oneself in bacon grease before an American, no?" Eleanor murmured, eyes dancing with laughter as she left, her hips swaying with each step.

Henry watched her exit for a moment before shaking his head, tearing his gaze from the woman. Only to blink as a hairy hand sneaked up, plucking a third kuih to deposit on the plate. He hissed a little at Tobias as he realized that the dessert was fast disappearing.

"Aye, lad. If you spend too much time watching one of those, you miss the more important things in life. Like the dessert before you," Tobias said with laugh, grabbing the last kuih he was missing from his plate before ducking backwards, using his sturdy bulk to push his way back to his seat. Once he was seated, he hunched over his meal with quiet, slow intensity.

"They're always like that," Jotun said, speaking to Henry as he reached over the man's head to pluck a single kuih pelita for his own consumption. "Trick you into thinking they're slow and careful. But then you take your eyes off them, and they make a move that will make a trickster spin."

"You'd know all about tricksters, now wouldn't you?" Marilyn said coolly.

Jotun just grinned before popping the entire kuih in his mouth, pandan leaf wrapping and all. Then, waving a hand in farewell, he headed out, dropping a pair of gold coins on the counter as he left, in payment. Amir's and Henry's gaze tracked the spinning gold coins, eyes wide with surprise.

"Did he just…?" Amir trailed off, shaking his head.

"Pretty sure he did." Henry gulped, clamping a hand down on his hand. He knew better than to even think about grabbing at the coins. Still…his fingers itched to pick the coins up and look them over. It was not as though he had a chance to handle such fine things very often.

Mo Meng seemed to find the matter completely unworthy of comment, having bid the man goodbye before returning to his kitchen. Kelly in the meantime had moved to bus their tables, bringing back plates and glasses of water before making the coins disappear behind the counter, out of temptation's path.

With the coins out of sight, Henry turned to the dessert tray, only to find the last piece being grabbed at by the Archmage and Lily. They were fighting over the last of the kuih lenggang, hands bumping into one another as they reached for it at the same time. It was the Archmage who managed to sneak it out from under the jinn's hand, longer fingers grabbing it first and leaving the jinn pouting.

"No fair."

"Life is rarely fair," the Archmage said, smirking. "Consider this payback, for our earlier discomfort." Turning on his heels, he strode out of the restaurant, gesturing for the pair of mages to catch up. Amir and Marilyn both glanced back toward the kitchen, at the empty tray, and then sighed, scurrying after him. It was only when Kelly managed to slip ahead of them, waving their bill, that they stopped.

Laughing a little, Henry shook his head as he watched the Archmage huffily pay his bill before leaving. Still, his amusement was short-lived as he stared at the empty tray. All his rubbernecking had definitely been to his detriment.

"I guess the dwarf was right…" Henry sighed, leaning back.

Only to have a plate pushed towards him. He frowned at the empty plate and the jinn who had nudged it over. Then, narrowing his eyes, he stared at the plate more fully. Hints of magic sparkled on it, magic that insisted he look away from the plate, that there was nothing there to be seen.

"A forget-me spell?" Henry snorted, finding the focal and anchor point of the spell with quick ease. He had used such magic before, when he had been gifted by the jinn. Breaking one apart was a matter of seconds, even one created by the jinn.

His prize…a single kuih in pandan leaf casing. "You shouldn't have…"

"I wouldn't. If you had missed it." Lily's smile danced on her lips, even as Kelly wandered over, hands on her hips.

"So, magic to stop monsters from beyond, to raise people up…and to hide dessert?" she said.

"What better use could there be, than to create happiness?"

For once, Henry chose not to answer or get involved, instead taking Tobias's advice and focusing on his meal.

After all, some things only came once in a lifetime.

FIFTEEN
Closing Up

Affter that, the rest of the night ended pretty fast. With a magically conjured rainstorm outside, blocking entrance and stymying business everywhere—and what kind of knock-on effects a single spell like that would have, Mo Meng did not even want to contemplate—he had chosen to close early after the last of his guests had left.

The last being Tobias, not the troublesome pair. Lily and Henry had wandered out, leaving a generous tip after settling their bill and then flickering away, the gentlest pull of magic putting them on the dragon lines and out of the city.

He approved of their caution, for while the Mage Council might have left with minimal issues, there were still those who hunted the jinn. Some to contain her, some to demand new wishes that she would not fulfill. Sometimes, Mo Meng felt the latest generation were more demanding, less prone to accept refusal than the generations before.

Then he reminded himself that he always came back to that thought, every couple of decades. Humanity changed, circumstances altered, but the core of people rarely differed. The challenges they faced, the burdens they had to overcome were just different. Each generation was but a reflection of their greatest burdens, and always, they improved.

Given a long enough view of time.

There were some generations, some decades that made Mo Meng despair, but those scars of war and disease and genocide; those scars also saw the greatest rise above them. And in time, improve upon the worlds before them.

He believed that. Had to believe it, to continue to live in this world after so many years. To work to improve it, in his own small ways.

Cooking, cleaning and hosting such gatherings.

"All clean, boss!" Kelly called, coming up to the counter and leaning against it. "Quiet night tonight. If a strange one."

"It was. And how are you? Disappointed?" he asked.

"With what?"

"Us. Magic," he shrugged. "That we cannot just wave a hand and fix the world."

She paused, considering his words and what he had stated. She picked at a stray hair that fell down the side of her face, twisting it around her finger for a moment before she let out a laugh. "Nah. I'm no child. There's no quick fix in this world.

"And I think, if you did fix it anyway, we'd fuck it up afterwards. When you all moved on, or died. Unless you became an immortal tyrant." She made a face. "And who wants one of those?"

"Even a benign tyrant?" Mo Meng said, amused. Remembering.

"Even a benevolent dictator is a dictator." She touched her chest. "I'm too much of a modern girl to not value freedom."

Mo Meng inclined his head. "Wisdom beyond your years, sometimes."

She laughed, rapping the table. "If that's all then, boss...transit's going to be a bitch with the rain."

He waved her out, watching her walk away. As she left, he was left with his own memories. Of a time when he himself tried to make the world better. Centuries, ruling over a small kingdom, one filled with magic and wonder and peace. An enforced peace.

And he turned his hands over, staring at them. Remembering how he had to create that peace, the sacrifices that had been made to ensure that war had never touched his paradise. A benevolent dictator was still a tyrant, and a murderous one if one was not under their care.

No.

This was better. A restaurant, meals that brought smiles. Meetings that resolved, because people talked things through.

He turned his head, taking in his surroundings. Though perhaps he would reduce the magic a little. Do some of this social media Kelly kept talking about. Maybe join the twentieth century.

Not the twenty-first. Mo Meng was not sure he was ready for that one, just yet.

But perhaps it was time to change. After all, a millennia-old jinn had done so.

###

THE END

Want to read more books set in this universe?

A sample chapter from A Gamer's Wish is included at the end of this book…

THE HIDDEN WISHES SERIES

WANT TO READ MORE ABOUT HENRY AND LILY?

One faithful day Henry Tsien finds a briefcase and a ring within it. Within hours, his world has changed as a helpful jinn introduces him to a hidden world. What can an old-school gamer given magic do in a world filled with age-old, hidden, supernatural creatures?

The Hidden Wishes series is an urban fantasy take on the GameLit genre. It is much lighter in terms of 'statistics' and its game system. This is the full trilogy of the series.

Books included:

A Gamer's Wish

A Squire's Wish

A Jinn's Wish

Enjoy the entire Hidden Wishes series in just one book!

www.starlitpublishing.com/products/ hidden-wishes-omnibus-books-1-3

AUTHOR'S NOTE

Thank you for reading the Nameless Restaurant novella. I've wanted to return to the Hidden Wishes universe for a bit and wanted to write a food book. I'd been playing with ideas for a bit, unsure of how or where to go, and then one day thought to put both of those desires together.

And out came the Nameless Restaurant.

I'm hoping you enjoyed the book. It was, in many ways, a labour of love for the writing, doing the research and putting together the recipes and everything else. Many of these dishes I've made myself so I can say for sure the recipes work, and should be incredibly tasty. In fact, the Gula Malacca Sago recipe is my go to when I have to bring something for a party—it's nut free, gluten free and dairy free which means that it bypasses a lot of concerns. Just remember, keep stirring!

But seriously, thank you for reading this. I hope you enjoyed Mo Meng and the Nameless Restaurant as much as I enjoyed writing it. The book is written to be a standalone, but depending on reception (and time!), I might return to the world again for another novella, building upon another incident and another series of tasty dishes.

~ Tao

ABOUT THE AUTHOR

Tao Wong is a Canadian author based in Toronto who is best known for his System Apocalypse post-apocalyptic LitRPG series and A Thousand Li, a Chinese xianxia fantasy series. His work has been released in audio, paperback, hardcover and ebook formats and translated into German, Spanish, Portuguese, Russian and other languages. He was shortlisted for the UK Kindle Storyteller award in 2021 for his work, A Thousand Li: the Second Sect. When he's not writing and working, he's practicing martial arts, reading and dreaming up new worlds.

Tao became a full-time author in 2019 and is a member of the Science Fiction and Fantasy Writers of America (SFWA) and Novelists Inc.

For updates on the series and his other books (and special one-shot stories), please visit the author's website:

www.mylifemytao.com

Subscribe to Tao's mailing list to receive exclusive access to short stories in the Thousand Li and System Apocalypse universes.

If you'd like to support Tao directly, he has a Patreon page—benefits include previews of all his new books, full access to series short stories, and other exclusive perks. Tao Wong Patreon:

www.patreon.com/taowong

For more great information about LitRPG series, check out these Facebook groups:

www.facebook.com/groups/LitRPGsociety

www.facebook.com/groups/LitRPG.books

ABOUT THE PUBLISHER

Starlit Publishing is wholly owned and operated by Tao Wong. It is a science fiction and fantasy publisher focused on the LitRPG & cultivation genres. Their focus is on promoting new, upcoming authors in the genre whose writing challenges the existing stereotypes while giving a rip-roaring good read.

For more information on Starlit Publishing, visit our website!

www.starlitpublishing.com

You can also join Starlit Publishing's mailing list to learn of new, exciting authors and book releases.

RECIPES FROM THE NAMELESS RESTAURANT

Golden Fried Rice

Ingredients
2 cups of cooked, day-old rice
½ teaspoon of salt
4 egg yolks
½ tablespoon high grade soya sauce
1 teaspoon Shaoxing rice wine
½ teaspoon sesame oil
Dash of white pepper (optional)
2 cloves of garlic, finely chopped
1 large yellow onion
(or substitute for 2 scallions)
3 tablespoons of sunflower oil

Garnish

Cilantro
Deep fried, crispy slices of garlic
(to taste)

Instructions

1. Prep and set aside all ingredients beforehand. Onions (or shallots) and garlic should be chopped finely, to allow for quick cooking. If you are using deep fried garlic slices, slice into 1 mm thick slices and deep-fry beforehand and set aside to cool. Break and split egg whites and yolk. Keep egg whites for other dishes or as a wash.

2. In a medium bowl, add the chilled, day-old rice and egg yolks and salt. Mix gently until every grain is coated. There should be no lumps or chunks of rice. If you are having issues with lumps, it is often because the rice is too moist and/or cold. Allow the rice to come up

closer to room temperature before mixing further. Set aside.

3. Bring your wok (or large frying pan) to a high temperature. It should just begin to smoke, before you add the sunflower oil. Do not use olive oil or other low smoke point oils (that includes fats and butter) for this dish.

4. Add garlic and onions to the dish, begin stir frying. When the aroma of the garlic and onions can be smelt (should not take longer than a few seconds); add the mixed rice. Be careful of splatter and mess!

5. Begin stir-frying the ingredients together, keeping the rice moving. Add the Shaoxing rice wine, soya sauce and sesame oil to the pan. These 'wet' ingredients can be added to the rice beforehand while mixing the yolk if you find it too stressful to do so while stir-frying but make sure not to let it soak too long in that case.

6. Rice should dry fast if appropriately dry. Too wet rice will take too long to dry, thus leaving portions of it burnt or clumpy. Make sure to taste and add more salt, sesame oil or white pepper (optional) as needed.

7. Once rice is dry, extract from wok and plate. Garnish with cilantro and garlic chips.

Char Kuey Teow
(Pork, Chicken, or Vegetable)

Ingredients

Sauce
2 tablespoons soy sauce
1 tablespoon dark soy sauce
½ tablespoon oyster sauce
½ tablespoon fish sauce
(can be excluded if using blood cockles
below)
1 teaspoon sugar
½ teaspoon white pepper
(substitute white for black if you are
missing white pepper, but reduce
portions a little)

Cooking ingredients
180 grams of flat rice noodles
2 tablespoons of pork lard/high heat oil
1 chopped garlic clove
Half of a fish cake
1 egg
Half of a Chinese sausage
(dried Chinese sausage)
1 tablespoon chili paste (or to taste)
¼ cup of fresh blood cockles
4 deveined large freshwater prawns
Sliced chives
Bean sprouts (to taste)

Instructions

1. Soak the flat rice noodles in water to separate the noodles. Mo Meng would recommend non-hardened, filter water or spring water.

2. Pre-make the sauce by adding sauce ingredients in a separate bowl. Mix together and set aside in easy reach of the wok. You can also make large batches of the

sauce for future cooking sessions. Store in the refrigerator.

3. Bring wok (or sauce pan) to high temperature, just as it is smoking. Do not add lard or oil till it is smoking.

4. Add oil or lard.

5. Immediately add the garlic cloves and the Chinese sausage. Saute till fragrant.

6. Add in freshwater prawns and stir fry until colour just changes (about 20-30 seconds). Add in fish cakes and saute for another brief period.

7. Add noodles and spoonfuls of the sauce. Once colour has begun to change, add the chili paste (amount to taste) in a corner. Preheat the chili paste a little before mixing with the noodles. Wait until the dish is fragrant.

8. Add the egg in a corner of the wok. Break the egg yolk and mix into the noodles.

9. Finally, add the chives and bean sprouts, stir-frying until both are cooked.

10. Immediately plate and serve. Enjoy!

Curry Laska
(Chicken or Vegetable. Includes prawns)

Ingredients

Laska Paste

    1 teaspoon shrimp paste
    2 tablespoons dried shrimp (soak in hot water before combining)
    3-5 large dried chillis (soak in hot water before combining)
    2 fresh chillis
    6 garlic cloves
    3-5 shallots
    3 tablespoons galangal (ginger variant)
    6 candlenuts
    2 large lemongrass stalks
    2 teaspoons turmeric

2-3 cloves of crushed star anise
1 teaspoon ground cumin

Note, you can buy Laksa Paste from Asian grocery markets. Look for brands like Por Kwan, Ayam or Prima Taste. These are good brands for the paste and will give a more authentic taste. Try all of them to see which suits your taste bud.

Further note, the ingredients and ratios in laksa paste can vary depending on taste. Additional ingredients not mentioned can include coriander, paprika, fennel and fenugreek.

Ingredient for Laksa Broth (for 2)

2-3 tablespoons coconut oil
2 cups chicken broth
1 cup water
2-3 tablespoons laksa paste
400g (14 oz/1 can) of coconut milk (Santan)
2 lime leaves
Lime Juice (to taste if lime leaves are not available and/or you prefer more sour laksa types)

Fish sauce (to taste and can be excluded if you are using bloody cockles!)

Ingredients (for 2)

50 grams of rice vermicelli
50 grams of hokkien noodles
(may be swapped, see notes below)
160 grams of shredded boiled chicken meat
80g of tofu puffs (2-4 per person)
80g of bean sprouts
4-8 large deveined and peeled shrimps
2 lightly cooked eggs (split in half)
2 large tablespoons of blood cockles

Instructions

To Make Laksa Paste:

1. Soak the dried shrimps and dried chillis in hot water for 10-15 minutes before processing.
2. Grind cumin, star anise and turmeric (if purchased dried).

3. Chop all other wet ingredients –
   garlic, shallots, galangal, fresh
   chillis, lemongrass and candlenuts
   before throwing in food processor.
   Grind quickly and roughly.
   Tip – for a tasty but not spicy
   experience, make sure to pull out the
   chili seeds beforehand from both fresh
   and dried chilis. Reduce the number
   too (3-4 chilis for a milder experience,
   5-6 for a spicier one).

4. Add in the shrimp paste and the
   soaked dried shrimps and chillis
   into the food processor along with
   the fried.

5. Grind until a vibrant paste is
   created. You can batch process this
   and store in a cool dry place for
   months.

To Make Laksa Broth

1. Boil chicken broth and water together. You can cook your chicken in the chicken broth and water together to save time. You can also grill the chicken if you wish, though the preference generally is to boil.

2. Heat oil and when it is warm, add the tablespoons of laksa paste within. Fry until fragrant (2-3 minutes) and then set aside to be added to the chicken broth above.

3. Add the coconut milk and lime leaves.

4. Add the fish sauce (if you are missing the blood cockles) and lime juice to taste.

5. Add tofu puffs for meal.

6. Boil and then lower to a simmer.

To Assemble Laksa

1. Boil a large pot of water.
2. Add shrimp to laksa broth and cook for 2-3 minutes.
3. Meanwhile, cook noodles in this separate pot of water. 2-3 minutes in general. There are two types of noodles listed, preference for type of noodles is individual. Hokkien noodles take longer, maifan (vermicelli noodles) cook faster. Check directions.
4. Place noodles in bowl.
5. Add fresh blood cockles to bowl along with shredded chicken.
6. Pour laksa broth, shrimp and tofu puffs over the noodles.
7. Add the split egg (one per bowl) and bean sprouts.
8. Garnish with fresh limes or mint.
9. Serve with chili sauce and lime wedges.

Sago and Gula Malacca
(Gluten & Lactose Free)

Ingredients

10 cups of water

7 ounces of sago pearls (sago balls that are tiny)

2 cups of coconut milk

7 ounces of gula malacca (processed palm sugar) & ½ cup of water

Instructions

1. Bring water to boil over stove. Make sure this is a rolling boil.

2. Slowly add the sago pearls to the boiling water. Continually stir the water and sago balls so that they do not clump together or stick to the bottom. Lower heat to low.

3. Sago balls are done when the pearls are entirely clear. Takes 20-30 minutes. The more water you have, the easier this will be.

4. Strain sago through a fine sieve to remove excess water. Transfer to jelly molds and/or dessert cups. Refrigerate contents overnight.

5. In a small saucepan, prepare the gula malacca (Melaka) syrup. To do this, break up palm sugar into small chunks. Gradually add the half cup of water over low heat, stirring to dissolve the sugar. Bring to a boil and keep stirring until sugar is entirely dissolved. Thicken to desired consistency – generally a light syrup. Strain through light mesh to remove grit.

6. Unmold sago. Serve on plates (or in cups). Serve coconut milk and syrup separately, to allow each person to pour to desired taste.

PREVIEW OF A GAMER'S WISH:
Book 1 of Hidden Wishes

Simple curiosity. That was all it took to change my world.

My life changed with a black briefcase one spring evening. It had a 1960s design, a perfect rectangle made of black leather with a number-combination lock, still in pristine condition. It was the fifth and last piece of luggage I had purchased earlier that day at the lost luggage auction—and the most expensive piece. Unless I was really lucky, I might make enough for a week's groceries from all this. At some point, I knew that I had to find a new job, but lucky for me, retail jobs were a dime a dozen right now. If you were willing to take late-night shifts at least. Still, that was a concern for future me.

Luggage like this always left me wondering about its story. The smell of the leather, the faintest hint as I held it to my nose, told me it was probably genuine.

Maybe it was a hipster throwback, a handmade piece for people with more money than sense, but something told me it was the real deal. A genuine 1960s briefcase. That raised a number of questions: Was it an old purchase, set aside and never used till recently? Perhaps given to a new graduate, a present to commemorate their graduation? Did someone buy it at a thrift store, a discarded piece of luggage that wasn't wanted or needed till it was unceremoniously lost and abandoned again? That was, after all, how it had come into my possession. The airport auctioned off uncollected lost luggage every sixty days after it entered the system.

I sat silently for a time as I ran my hands along the briefcase and made up stories about its former owner, the briefcase, and what I might find within. Small stories, daydreams of the kinds of things I'd find inside—a laptop, a journal, maybe a calculator for an accountant. Business cards, of course. It was a briefcase. I took my time because this was half the fun of buying lost luggage—the stories I got to make up before the inevitable disappointment of reality. And while I thought, I ran my fingers along the numerical lock and attempted to open the case.

Click.

Four-six-seven. I idly noted the number that worked before I continued my attempts on the opposite side. It took another two minutes, an impatient two minutes as I found myself suddenly anxious to see what I had bought. When the click came, I held my breath for a second before I finally opened the briefcase to see my prize.

A leather journal, a single, expensive-looking fountain pen, and a capped bottle of ink snuggly fit into an inkwell dominated one side of the briefcase. On the other side, a series of nine small boxes with carved runes on top of them sat in what had to be a custom-made enclosure. I frowned as I traced the runes, never having seen anything like them before. Not that I was any expert, mind you, but they sure were pretty. On the underside of the top of the briefcase was a simple, silver-lined mirror that reflected my image to me.

Wavy brown hair that was about two weeks overdue for a haircut, slanted brown eyes that I had been told were my best feature and thin lips reflected back at me. I rubbed my chin, realizing I had forgotten to shave again and grown a sparse, stubbly goatee. It was a bad habit, but shaving was never a priority when you only had to do it every few weeks. Just another gift of being ethnically southern Chinese. At twenty-eight, I was glad I'd finally gotten out of the "baby face" period of my life, even if I was still occasionally mocked for looking like I was in my early twenties. That was okay, considering some of those same mockers were already losing their hair.

Initial perusal over, I began the process of stripping the briefcase. I started with the book first and found, to my surprise, it was empty. Nothing was on the front page or any of the succeeding pages. It had very nice binding though and high-quality leather. I'd probably make a few dollars selling it online. The fountain pen was an old dip-and-write type, might have been worth something to a collector. I capped the pen and put it away carefully. The ink I pulled out and set aside with the rest of the junk. No money in reselling used ink.

Lastly, I started opening the boxes. And that's when things started getting weird. The first box held scales; the second, a series of dead beetles; the third, feathers from a single type of bird; and the fourth, old, dark earth. After the second box, I grabbed the garbage and started tossing contents into it immediately. Perhaps this had been owned by a taxidermist? Or a naturalist?

"Oww!" I howled and shook my hand. When I had touched the fifth box, what must have been the accumulated static charge of living in a basement apartment had shocked me. It had never been that bad before, but I made a mental note to get a humidifier...when I had the money.

Gingerly, I touched the box and, finding the charge gone, I opened it, ready to toss its contents away. Instead, I found a simple signet ring made of a dark metal. Or alloy of metals. I frowned as I plucked the ring out and rubbed at it to clean it up, curious to see what it was made of.

As I said, curiosity changed my life.

"Are you done yet?" the blond woman, who had formed in my apartment from smoke, asked me. Clad in a pink bra, tiny vest, and billowy sheer pants, she reminded me of an actress from an old, cheesy TV show, almost uncannily so. Seriously, the blond genie that stood in front of me with her sardonic smile would have sent copyright lawyers salivating at the fees they'd earn. If they could have seen her. And if she hadn't wished them away.

"You...you're a genie! But that was a ring, not a lamp!" I spluttered, the ring that the smoke had streamed from still clutched in my hand in a death grip.

"Jinn! And yes, I am. What may I do for you, Master?" the genie said. Turning her head, she looked around my bachelor suite with a flicker of distaste. "Maybe a bigger residence?"

"You're a genie…" I stared at the blonde, my mind caught in a circular trap as it struggled with the insanity in front of it. After all, genies didn't exist. But there, in front of me, was a genie.

"Oh, hell. I really can't wait for this entire 'enlightenment' period to be over," the genie said with a roll of her eyes after I just continued to stare at her blankly. She turned away from me and walked around the room before she stopped at my micro-kitchen to open the fridge. Bent over, she fished inside before extracting day-old fried rice and popping a bite into her mouth. A conjured spoon later, she was digging into last night's dinner and prodding my stove, flat-screen TV, and laptop. "What is this?"

"Fried rice."

"I know what fried rice is. And this isn't bad," she complimented me, ignoring my mumbled thanks while she pointed at the TV screen and then laptop. "This. And this."

"TV and laptop."

"Huh." She returned to the TV before she prodded at it a few more times and inevitably adjusted its angle. "That's amazing. I guess your science actually does have some use. Well, outside of indoor plumbing. That isn't as good."

My brain finally stopped going in circles after I decided to stop trying to actually understand what was going on. If I had a genie in my house, I had a genie. "So, your name isn't Jeannie, is it?"

"Do I look like a Jeannie to you?"

"Well…"

"The Seven Seals!" The genie flickered, and the previously blonde creature transformed into a black-haired, hawk-nosed Middle-Eastern woman…with considerably less clothing than before, which should have been a challenge. "Call me Lily. What's yours?"

"Uhh…"

"Aaargh!" Lily stared at her clothing and then stared at me for a moment. A second later, she was clad in a T-shirt that said "I Aim to Misbehave" and a pair of jeans. I would admit I found the new clothing options even more distracting, especially since they were an exact replica of what I was wearing.

"I'm Henry. And what was that about?"

"Nothing. Nothing at all," Lily snapped at me and waved her spoon at my laptop. "What is a 'laptop'?"

"A portable computer," I explained.

"No, I've seen a computer before. They take up rooms three times the size of your…residence," Lily said, prodding my laptop.

"Computers haven't been that big since the fifties. Okay, maybe sixties. And I guess there are supercomputers that are that big these days," I blathered on. "But most people don't really need a supercomputer. I mean, all I do with mine is play some games and get on the Internet."

"Internet?" Lily raised her spoon. "Wait. Stop. Two things: what year is this, and do you have more food?"

"Twenty eighteen, and there's some pizza in the freezer," I said. "What year did you think this was?"

"That explains why the enchantments have faded," Lily said as she finished raiding my fridge. She stared at the pizza and then looked at me imploringly. I sighed and helped her add it to the microwave, which I then had to explain to her. That certainly dated her further, putting her at least into the 1960s, which was around the same time as the briefcase. Once the pizza was ready and the genie was eating, I got back to the important questions.

"What enchantments?"

"All of them, of course. They really should have closed off the runes between the concealment and defensive enchantments. If they'd asked me, I could have told them. But of course, they never do," Lily said, shaking her head. "Once the enchantment wasn't being regularly recharged, the concealment rune started draining the rest. Took it about fifty years or so, at a guess. Good thing for you they were sloppy; otherwise, you'd be dead."

"Dead?"

"Oh, yes. Heart attack when you failed the third time on opening the briefcase," Lily said. "Always a good defensive spell—few creatures can survive without a heart. Well, except the undead, but they wouldn't be able to even touch the briefcase with the wards against them."

"I could have died," I said weakly as I stumbled to my bed and sat down with a thud.

"Blazing suns." Lily sat down across from me. "You humans are always so damn sensitive about your mortality."

I sat there in silence and stared at the far wall, my brain refusing to work any further at this new revelation.

Genies. Magic. My death. There is a certain point in an individual's day when one just can't go on, and I'd hit that point. Without speaking, I flopped onto my bed, grabbed my comforter, and rolled into a ball.

When I woke hours later, the sun had set, and my basement apartment was shrouded in darkness. I exhaled in relief, grateful but slightly disappointed that the blond/brunette genie had been but a weird dream. Paper rustled, and I twisted my head to the side to spot a pair of glowing red eyes bent over a book.

"Well, that was a very manly scream," Lily said, hiding a smirk.

"You...what are you doing?" I gulped, clutching my comforter to my body after I finally managed to turn on my bedside light. The additional illumination drove the fire from her eyes, making them look human again. I recalled the flames that lit her face from within, doubting I'd ever forget them. Not demonic though...at least, they didn't feel demonic. Just otherworldly.

"Hmmm? Reading. You have quite a selection here." Lily nodded to the bookcases that lined the walls of my apartment. I will admit books are one of my indulgences. The books are wide ranging, covering everything from history to fiction. Really, I just grabbed whatever seemed interesting when I hit a garage sale.

"It wasn't a dream," I muttered to myself and put my head between my knees.

"Yes, yes. Are you going to have a breakdown again, or are we finally getting to the part where you make a wish?" Lily said, bored. "If you want to wait, I've still got two books in this series to finish."

"Don't bother. The author's still not done book six after six years. So magic really is real?" I said, my voice muffled by the comforter. "And you're a genie. Like, 'rub the lamp and get three wishes' kind of genie."

"Yes, and I'm a jinn, not a genie, and sort of," Lily said absently as she continued to read.

"Sort of?" I latched on to the wishy-washy word.

"I'm not actually bound to fulfill all three wishes since what I can do is limited by the ring and my powers," Lily said and then, when I said nothing, looked up and explained further. "If you wished for the sun to go out, I wouldn't be able to do it, and you'd have wasted my power in trying. And annoyed like a hundred gods at the same time. I am also bound to the ring, not a lamp, unlike what Antoinne might have written."

"Antoinne?" I shook my head. No. I was not going to get distracted. It was hard enough keeping my head on straight. "Magic is real." I could not keep the wonder from my voice as I said that. In a world of mediocrity and the mundane, magic was real.

"Always has been."

"But how did I not know of it?"

"Your world of science and rational thought blinded you to the arcane. What cannot be explained was relegated to hidden corners of the world, and rare as the gift is, it is no wonder humanity forgot. Magic is still practiced in back alleys and small towns. The supernatural world still exists, but it is more than happy to be forgotten. After all, humanity has never been kind to what it considers others."

"You've given that speech before," I said, and Lily nodded. "All right then, so magic is real, and you're a ge—" At her pointed stare, I corrected myself. "Jinn, and I have three wishes. Is there anything I shouldn't wish for?"

"Life. Death. The fate of countries. Time travel. I can alter the minds and physical reactions of others but not their souls; I cannot make someone love you or stop hating you, just lust for you or perhaps temper their physical reactions to your presence," Lily answered promptly. As I nodded along, she opened her mouth and then shut it.

"You were going to say something."

"I was."

"What was it?"

"It doesn't matter."

"Why not?" I leaned forward in my chair. I wished the light shone better on her face. At least then I would have a better view of it. There was something in her voice.

Lily stayed silent for a time, obviously fighting something internally. In the end, her lips twisted wryly, and she waved a hand in front of my bookcases, causing them to glow slightly. "Because you won't listen."

"That's a bit insulting. You don't know me," I said, and she laughed, her laughter brittle and high.

"I know you. I've known a hundred thousand like you. My masters never listen," Lily said with a smile. "So tell me your wish."

I almost snapped back that I wished she would tell me what she was going to say. Almost. But annoyed or not, I was not going to waste my chance at real magic, at a real chance to change my world. "You don't know me, and I don't know you. So why don't you tell me, and maybe, maybe we'll come to know one another."

Lily stared at me for a long time, her eyes glowing red before she finally spoke, her voice weary. "I am bound by the ring to fulfill your wishes, but I am not omniscient. I can only change what I understand, and I am not responsible for the consequences of any changes. Not that it'll stop you from blaming me."

I stared at Lily for a time, then slowly nodded. "You're saying if I made a wish, you'd be forced to make it happen even if it was a silly wish. Like, if I wished for a million dollars right this second, you'd be forced to make it appear right in this room. Maybe as bills, maybe as dollar coins, which probably would suck."

"I am not malicious, no matter what you people might say," Lily said. "But most wishes for wealth are not well thought out. I once gave a goatherder a mountain of gold, and he and his family were killed for it. A hundred years ago, a gentleman asked for a million pounds. Of course, I had never seen the kind of notes they used, so I made the bank notes for him, a million dollars' worth, all exactly the same. He was unhappy about that."

I slowly nodded, staring at her. "You're not all-powerful and all-knowing, just powerful. Like a giant hammer wielded by toddlers."

"Yes!" Lily said, excited for a second.

I grunted, closing my eyes. The worse part was that I was the damn toddler. But still…magic was real.

I had not realized I had spoken that thought aloud till that whisper echoed through the basement. Into the silence, she slowly spoke. "Do you desire magic then?"

"With every fiber of my being," I answered honestly. "But I can see a million, billion ways it could go wrong. Wish for magic, and I might get the ability without the knowledge to wield it. Wish for knowledge and ability, and you'd stick it all in my head and maybe make me go crazy while doing it. Wish for a mentor, and, well, it might be a black mage who comes in."

"You did listen." Lily's lips twisted into a wry smile. "Though, again, not directly malicious. If you wished for the knowledge to wield magic, and that alone, I'd probably only insert enough that you would not be driven mad."

"You can do that?" I blinked, having rattled off my words without thought. I hadn't actually expected her to know how to inject information into my head.

"Of course. I'm a jinn who has been in the service of some of the greatest mages this world has ever known. I am no dotard myself," Lily boasted. "Adding knowledge direct would be no different than creating a magical book of learning. In fact, it would be simpler without the preservation and containment spells."

"Huh," I said, rubbing my chin and staring at the girl. "So, it's not the amount of knowledge but the speed."

"Close enough," she said, and I grunted.

"I guess I'd have to level up first."

"Level up?" Lily asked, and I waved my hand toward my bookshelf where my RPG books were neatly stacked from D&D's first editions to more recent RPGs, indie and mainstream publishers. "One second." She muttered that word and then shimmered for a brief moment, a second at most, and suddenly all the books were stacked neatly around her. "How interesting. Entire universes written and governed by rules and dice."

"Did you just read all of them with super speed?" I asked.

"Not super speed. That's always more trouble than its worth. You have to deal with friction and air resistance and heat. I prefer to slow time," Lily said nonchalantly. "I do see what you mean. These 'levels' characters have limit their growth, giving them knowledge and strength as they pass each milestone."

"You're saying it's possible? For me to wield magic if we put it in a game system?" I said excitedly, fallen hopes rising again like a rocket at her words.

"Of course. Who do you think you're talking to?" Lily asked.

"Perfect!" I paused, frowning as I worked out the implications. Perhaps I had found a way to cheat the system. "All right. One last question - how do I know everything you've said is true?"

At those words, even in the dim light, I saw Lily's face twist with quickly concealed hurt. She looked away for a second and then back at me. "Well, that's the rub, isn't it? You can't."

That was the rub. It wasn't as if I could look this up on Snopes or jump on Quora, seeking expert advice. The stories I did know of, they conflicted. The original stories of jinn said they were like us, neither good nor evil, creatures of free will like humanity itself. Since then, they'd been both friend and foe in a myriad of stories. Of course, it wasn't as if I knew how to tell which were true or fake.

In the end, it came down to trust. Could I, should I, trust Lily? Did it matter though? By her own admission, anything I wished for needed her interpretation. Of course that too could have been a lie. But for a chance at magic, however slim it might be, I would take it.

With that thought, I smiled and leaned forward. "All right, so here's what I was thinking."

Read more about Harry and Lily in the completed Hidden Wishes series!

www.starlitpublishing.com/products/ a-gamers-wish

Made in the USA
Las Vegas, NV
29 June 2023